Quiet Boy

A 1962 Selection of the

WEEKLY READER
Children's Book Club
Education Center • Columbus 16, Ohio

QUIET BOY

by

LELA AND RUFUS WALTRIP

ILLUSTRATIONS BY
THERESA KALAB SMITH

DAVID McKAY COMPANY, INC.
NEW YORK

WEEKLY READER
Children's Book Club
Edition, 1962

QUIET BOY

LIBRARY OF CONGRESS CATALOG CARD NUMBER 61–7882

Printed in the United States of America
By American Book-Stratford Press, Inc., N.Y.

Contents

Quiet Boy

1: *Sheep's Tail*

THE LATE evening sun was sinking behind the red cliffs of Arizona's Canyon de Chelly when the school bus drew up at the Navajo Trading Post. It was Friday, five days since Sunday.

"Hurry up there. Let's get going!" shouted the Indian boys and girls as they pushed and shoved, pouring out of the long yellow school bus stopped beside the highway.

Quiet Boy sat still and waited. He always waited. He was always the last one off and the last one on. He said nothing.

"Come on, sheep's tail—Quiet One," called Pepe, son of Many Goats. "Let's have a game of marbles before your mother comes for you."

Quiet Boy grinned good-naturedly. He knew Pepe's nickname for him was with good intent. Chee was his real Indian name—Chee, son of Ditsa Toddy. He got up then and followed the others to the front. He fondled the marbles in his blue-jeans pocket. There was one thing he could do best—win at marbles. He took out the small black agate and looked at it. It held magic for him. He was sure of it. Soon he would prove this. He would carry home a pocket full of these magic gems, that is, if Nespah didn't come for him too soon. And she would not, for his mother had much to do at the hogan at the end of the week.

The slanting rays of the setting sun glinted on the smooth, polished black agate in his hand. Quiet Boy would almost as soon have lost his turquoise-studded belt as that black-agate taw. And the turquoise in the wide silver concho belt had been left him by his father, Ditsa Toddy. It was said to be worth upward of a hundred dollars. He had made the concho belt himself. From the true bright silver he had hammered it, guided by the experienced hand of Grandfather. In the silver buckle he had put the turquoise shaped like a Thunderbird, for the Thunderbird was a good omen.

"The blue stone will ward off danger and sickness," Nespah had told him, when he had finished the belt.

Quiet Boy had wondered about his mother's teaching. Why had not the blue stone kept his father from danger? Why had he not come back from the white man's war across the seas, since the turquoise was on his dog chain around his neck? He wanted so much to know, to understand. But all Nespah could say was, "That is what we have been taught. It is the Navajo way."

But that was not enough. Quiet Boy wished to know more. Was his mind tricking him? Would the government school teach him these things? He was in the seventh grade now and he had learned many things already but he had not learned this.

"Black Chiddi, Black Chiddi!" someone cried, and all the boys ran at once to an old black automobile that had driven up beside the Trading Post.

There was great excitement connected with that rattling, rusty, black car. The driver, Black Chiddi, as he had become known, was a teller of tales. True or untrue, the tales were fascinating.

Quiet Boy put the agate in his pocket and ran to catch up with the others.

"And you, sheep's tail, what did you learn at the school today?" Black Chiddi pointed a long crooked finger at Quiet Boy as he came up. "Did you learn how to shear a sheep? Did you learn to weave a Navajo blanket better than your grandmother?"

"E-c-c-c-c-!" shouted Tall Boy in delight, and a yell went up from the group as they slapped their sides in laughter.

Quiet Boy's ears turned a reddish-purple like the tall cliffs of Canyon de Chelly. His friends could call him sheep's tail, yes, but Black Chiddi— He started to speak but caught himself in true Navajo fashion. "Hold your tongue," Grandfather always said. "It is well to teach what we think is right but not with angry words or with force of blows."

He thrust his hands deep into his pockets. He could not look up. The black agate seemed to turn over in his clenched fist. He was plainly confused. Black Chiddi turned to the others then with a satisfied air.

"Did you learn how the great Kit Carson and his soldiers drove the Navajos out of their own land that had been theirs for centuries? Did they show you a movie of the white men burning the hogans of the Dineh, the people, destroying our flocks and our horses?"

"We had the best horses in the land!" Tall Boy shouted.

"And the best horsemen!" Pepe cried.

"And the best—" other voices began and broke off as all eyes turned toward the Trading Post.

"What's going on here?" Jack Burns, nephew of the trader, came to the edge of the group. He put his arms across the shoulders of Quiet Boy and Pepe and peered over at Black Chiddi sitting there in the black car with the ragged top down.

Abruptly, Black Chiddi decided he had said enough. He turned on the ignition switch, stepped on the gas, and pulled away. The boys fell back with sly glances and moved off as the car roared toward the highway.

"*Ya hoi!* Until next time!" some of them shouted after him in Navajo and in English.

"Another one of his wild stories," Pepe told Jack as they walked back to the Trading Post. "He is always talking about Black Horse of long ago, and how he came to blows with the white man over the schools."

"True or untrue," Quiet Boy added, shrugging indifferently, glad to be rid of the man. He had never liked the troublemaker and now he did not like him at all.

"Maybe so true," Tall Boy said.

"Let's go!" Pepe ran forward a little, squatting to make a round circle in the dry earth with his fingers.

"Play?" Quiet Boy looked at Jack as he took the marbles from his jeans pockets.

"Sure," said Jack, squatting beside the circle.

Then Quiet Boy saw it. His mother's green-covered wagon topped the hill and rolled leisurely down the long flat road toward the Trading Post. On the seat beside her sat his younger brother, eight-year-old Atchee. He could see the head of his younger sister, Ti-wi, bob up and down in the back of the wagon as it bounced over the rough road. Gogo, the sheep dog, trotted behind with tongue out, seeing everything, saying nothing, very much like Quiet Boy.

"Later," Quiet Boy called to the boys. Putting the marbles back into his pocket, he ran out to meet his family.

Nespah, smiling, stopped the wagon to let him in. But before the ponies were drawn up, while the wagon was still rolling, Quiet Boy grasped the side boards, put one

foot on the brake beam and threw himself over. His
family was smiling. How glad they were to see him and
he to see them!

"You are too big already," Ti-wi said laughing.

"You do look as though you had grown in these five
days," Nespah said.

Standing straight and tall in the wagon behind the
spring seat, arms folded on his chest, Chee, son of Ditsa
Toddy, rode on down to the Trading Post. He gave
Gogo a pat on the head, and they all went into the store
to do their weekly trading.

Over her shoulder, Nespah carried the orange-and-purple rug that she had just finished. Ti-wi, who was only ten, two years younger than Quiet Boy, carried another rug, similar only smaller. Atchee took in the silver-and-turquoise bracelet he had fashioned by hand with the help of his grandfather.

Quiet Boy gazed proudly at the weaving and at the silversmith work. If the trader thought it was good, he would pay them well for it, for he had proved to be an honest man and his tongue was straight. The boy drew himself up to his full height, tall for twelve years, and went forward to meet the trader. He had been there many times before but always his mother had taken the lead. Now he was almost a man. Hadn't he been going to government school for two months? Wasn't he in the seventh grade?

"You are a big boy now," Nespah had told him only five days ago. "You have learned to read and write. You speak the English well. It is time to take your father's place."

This had been a great responsibility for so small a boy. But Grandfather was old. No one knew how old. And so he, Quiet Boy, would have to do it.

"What is to be done, is to be done," Nespah always said. "Many words won't change things."

Often before he had hung back. He had followed his family, but from today he was the leader. He remembered his mother's trust. He eyed the trader arranging some canned goods on the shelves and went slowly back to meet him.

"Want something, son?" The trader's voice startled him even though he had been waiting for him to speak.

"My—my family," the boy stammered and gestured toward them. "They have come to trade."

"Yes," the trader said, and went to help them.

Quiet Boy sighed with relief. He leaned shyly on the counter and watched as the trader examined the rugs and the bracelet and put out canned goods, dress material, sugar or "sweet salt," and flour for them to take out to the wagon.

Quiet Boy dawdled, inspecting the new electrical equipment on the shelves. It was truly bewitching. Grandfather called the radio a "witch box" and wanted no part of it. But someday, Quiet Boy was sure, they would have one. It seemed such a useful thing. Many Navajos owned them. That is, they owned those that worked with batteries. It was this kind that Quiet Boy wanted.

The sun was fast dropping out of sight behind the red cliffs when they came out of the Trading Post. The boys had all disappeared. Only a few Navajo men stood or squatted here and there in little groups and talked.

Nespah held her full skirts just so as she climbed to the wagon seat, and sat to the left side. Always before she had sat on the right side next to the brake handle.

She had driven the team of ponies and managed the brake when they went down long steep hills. Today she handed the reins to Quiet Boy who sat on the right. Quiet Boy knew what to do. He put his feet on the high front endgate, slapped the ponies with the reins, clucked his tongue and they were off. Back up the long, flat, bumpy road they went toward home.

Ti-wi and Atchee plied him with many questions in Navajo. "What did you learn at the school?" Ti-wi could hardly wait to find out. At first Quiet Boy was reluctant to talk. He was thinking of Black Chiddi and of Tall Boy.

"What did you learn in school?" Black Chiddi had asked. "Did they show you a movie of the white men burning the hogans of the Dinch?" The sound of the man's words rang in his ears. He shifted in the seat, slapped the ponies with the reins again. He would forget Black Chiddi.

"There were the English words," he told Ti-wi and Atchee.

"What English words?" Ti-wi interrupted.

Quiet Boy knew how impatient she was to learn about the white man's ways. Perhaps next month or the next, she, too, could start to school. It all depended on the sheep, how well they turned out at the market. It depended, too, on the *Yei-bi-chai,* the strong medicine of the Mountain Chant which lasted for nine days. It depended on how well the evil influences had been driven out—how well the gods were appeased.

"Home," he told her in his native tongue. "Home is the English word, like our mother's hogan. It is a place to eat, and to sleep—and to be happy."

"O'o, yes." Ti-wi laughed aloud, her eyes dancing. "It is true. Our hogan is a happy one."

"Happy, yes, except for one—" Quiet Boy hesitated, the English lesson forgotten. He was talking too much.

"One?" Ti-wi stood up in the green-covered wagon. She held on to the seat in front of her. She relished every moment of this, every word spoken. "Except for one?" she asked again in Navajo.

Quiet Boy waited for the thoughts to go away. But they did not go. Six black eyes were upon him. He could feel them in the evening dusk. He sat very still and looked straight ahead, straight up the road. The sound of a plane hummed high in the sky and died out. A tumbleweed danced grotesquely across the road and waited for them to pass. The walls of the canyon shone blood red in the last rays of the afternoon sun. Like battlements of the ancient gods, like great strongholds, they stood there mysterious and beckoning, waiting.

"Our father," he finally spoke out. "A hogan needs one." And the silence was broken.

"O'o, yes," Ti-wi answered.

"O'o, yes," Atchee repeated.

"Ugh." Nespah shifted her weight on the spring seat. "That is true. But what is, is. That is done. We must look to the future. You are here. The hogan now has a man." She had spoken the words again.

Something quivered around Quiet Boy's heart like a taut bowstring. He was proud, yes, but he was lonely, always lonely and afraid. He didn't know why pains stabbed him. He didn't know why he should be confused about the Navajo ways and the ways of his white brothers. If he could only make up his mind to follow one trail or the other! Disturbed he was, all over again, by Black Chiddi.

But he must be brave. No one must know he was afraid. He sat a little straighter on the seat. He clucked his tongue to the ponies. Sheep's tail—or man? His mind was made up. He would never be the sheep's tail again, that is, if he could help it.

The family began to plan for the week-end trip to the mesa to gather the small piñon nuts that fell out of the cones of the piñon pines. They would go early this year, very early, before the small black nuts were all gone. If he picked many nuts perhaps he could buy a witch box, a radio!

Then it was dark. They had only the stars to guide them, the stars and the instinct of the ponies. The little ponies could find the way home in the darkest night.

"Just give them the reins," Grandfather had told him once.

Grandfather was old but he knew many things. Quiet Boy loosened the reins in his hands. The long leather lines fell slack along the backs of the ponies and up over the wagon front. The ponies plodded steadily, surely, along the dark road. Their small hoofs clicked on the hard ground. Occasionally sparks flew from the rocks struck by the horses' hoofs and Quiet Boy wondered if this was a good omen. Were the gods on his side?

When it was time to turn off the big road onto the dim trail that led up to the hogan, the ponies turned off. Nespah nodded on the seat beside Quiet Boy, confident, sure of his ability to take them home. The young ones slept on blankets in the back. Not until they drew up at the hogan did anyone stir.

"Grandfather has made a light for us," Ti-wi whispered as they reached the door of their hogan. Through the cracks between the logs they could see it, and through the openings beside the door that faced the east, and through the one small window beside the door where shone the gold star.

"Ssh!" Nespah cautioned.

But the old man did not wake when they raised the rug that covered the door opening and went inside. He lay on his sheepskin at one side of the large, mud-plastered room.

"He is old and tired." Nespah shook her head as she went about preparing a meal for her hungry brood.

When Quiet Boy had put the ponies in the corral he joined his family around the center fireplace. His eyes took in the hogan at one glance. There was the sewing machine of which his mother was very proud. And there the "gold" bedstead with the soft mattress for his mother and Ti-wi. It had been a gift from his father. And a real table with chairs. There was an empty place between the bed and the machine. It would be a good place for a radio, if ever they had one. And there was his father's workbench with all the tools the silversmith would use, the hammers, the sandstone molds, the bellows, the ladle for heating the silver, files and sandpaper.

Soon the steaming meal was ready. The mutton stew and the store-bought bread tasted good, and Quiet Boy caught himself dipping into the bowl oftener than he really should.

Ti-wi flashed him a smile when he noticed that she was aware of this.

"The food at the government school was never so good," Quiet Boy told them, and saw his mother's face light up. She, too, had been to the school for a little while. She had tasted the food there, and thought it good.

"What is the food like at the school?" Ti-wi finally asked.

"There are many kinds," he told her.

"Like what?" she queried.

"They have milk and vegetables," he answered her. "There are eggs and cheese, and fresh raw things—carrots and lettuce. Jack says that is rabbit food." Quiet Boy grinned.

"I would like some rabbit food." Ti-wi laughed.

"We must sleep now," Nespah told them. "Tomorrow is the piñon hunt."

Sheepskins were unrolled and spread out around the wall of the log hogan for the boys. Quiet Boy took off his shoes and blue jeans and folded them to one side as he had been taught to do at school. But before he blew out the small kerosene lamp, he held it high above his head and studied the picture that had hung on the wall so long. Quiet Boy had been only five when it was first put up. The Marine, the third from the left in the picture, was his father, Ditsa Toddy. A lump filled the boy's throat as he blew out the light and lay down on his sheepskin bed.

2: *Piñon-Nut Hunting*

It was yellow dawn. The early morning sun spread its first rays through the open door of the hogan. Quiet Boy slipped quickly into his jeans, put on his shoes, and went out to the corral. He would have the ponies ready to go when breakfast was over. His heart hammered with excitement when he thought of it. Nut hunting was one of the most treasured times of the year. He wondered if his hands were too soft or his back too weak after two months in the school. He wondered if he could ever measure up to what Nespah and Grandfather expected of him. At least he would not be the sheep's tail this morning. He would go to the mesa early and bring back enough nuts to buy a radio. Quiet Boy chanted in Navajo as he worked:

> *"Ana yi a ana yi*
> *Ana yi e ya he ya yo."*

He threw a stick for Gogo to chase, and ran back to

the hogan from which came the good smell of cedar wood burning and meat cooking.

Soon a breakfast of mutton ribs cooked in corn meal was eaten. The rolls of sheepskin bedding and enough food for two days were loaded into the wagon along with a barrel of water, and they were off. Grandfather seemed as excited as the others even though he could not go.

"My fingers are stiff with rheumatism and my legs are slow." He smiled. "But I am still good for something. I will tend the sheep and guard the hogan."

"There are many of us," Nespah told him. "One will stay with you."

But the old one shook his head. "The Ancients' gods will stay with me. I am not alone. Besides, many hands pick many nuts." And he waved them off.

Quiet Boy sat high on the spring seat. The red bandana around his head flapped in the breeze. How good it was to be a Navajo driving his own horses, taking his family to the high mesa! Higher and higher went the long flat road. Nespah chanted a Navajo song and they all chimed in. Happiness seemed everywhere.

Gogo, the brown-and-white dog, led the way, trotting along in front of the ponies or yapping happily at their heels.

"Yap, yap!" he barked, leaping away after a cottontail rabbit, and soon came back carrying it in his mouth.

"He earns his keep." Quiet Boy laughed. Handing Nespah the reins, he jumped out to take the rabbit. "I must do my part now," he said.

Soon it was skinned and prepared for the evening meal. The skin was stretched and hung on the side of the wagon to dry in the sun. It would help make soft moccasins for Ti-wi or Atchee, or ornaments to sell at the Trading Post. There was plenty of meat left for Gogo—meat and bones. How Gogo liked to gnaw on bones!

Soon they were on their way once more. Gogo, full and contented, trotted under the wagon making use of the brief shade it created at the midday.

It seemed cooler in the high country. Dull gray clouds floated across the blue sky.

"Man-wind, the north wind, and snow will come soon," Quiet Boy said, thinking of Grandfather's words. And Nespah nodded in agreement.

Presently they began to see wagons of other Navajo families who had left their farms in the care of relatives and camped in the piñons for the nut-harvest season. Quiet Boy knew that tons of nuts would be gathered this year. He had heard the trader say that in one good year, when the crop was at its best in Arizona and New

Mexico, there had been gathered and shipped out more than half a million dollars' worth.

"There are more people this year, and earlier than ever before," Nespah said anxiously.

"Do not worry," Quiet Boy told her. "I know a secret place where there should be nuts in plenty."

"Hunger is killing me, my mother," Atchee finally cried, watching a Navajo family eating beside the road.

"Yes," said Ti-wi, "hunger is killing us."

"Pull over and stop," their mother said, smiling at Quiet Boy.

Soon they, too, were resting under a cottonwood tree beside the road, munching the sweet cakes that Nespah knew they all liked. Then they were on their way again with squeals of delight from Ti-wi and Atchee. Soon they would reach the secret place. Soon they would taste the sweet piñon nuts.

"*Ei-yei!*" called a familiar voice and there was Doli beside a juniper tree. Doli was the daughter of Yellow Corn and Many Goats, who were their closest neighbors.

"*Ei-yei!*" exclaimed Ti-wi as the wagon rolled along. She was Doli's own age. "You come early to gather piñon nuts."

"Yes," said Doli, "and you, yourself, came early. And all the others." They laughed at the joke and Doli went back to gathering nuts, putting them into a flour sack.

Doli was dressed in full Navajo costume, for this was

a special occasion as well as a time for nut gathering. Her green velvet skirt fell in heavy folds, banded in yellow braid. Her jacket was red velvet, and a many-colored Pendleton blanket hung about her shoulders. Around her neck and waist were heavy silver and turquoise. Red-brown moccasins hugged her small feet. Quiet Boy's eyes followed Doli with shy delight. How glad he was that she and Ti-wi were friends!

He knew that her father, Many Goats, had been his father's friend, his "buddy" in the war. Only her father had returned—with many scars on his body and a limp, yes, but he had returned. He had brought wonderful stories back to the hogans, stories of danger and of bravery.

Quiet Boy had heard these stories over and over. He had not tired of hearing about the many Navajo Marines in the South Pacific, in Sicily, Italy, Africa, and in the Aleutian Islands. Theirs had been an unusual job—code talking in the Signal Corps. This meant that two Navajos would speak to each other by radio or telephone, giving military messages in their own language, straight across enemy lines. This was a unique service he had been told. The enemy could never guess the meaning of the Indian language—his father's language.

His father had gone to school to the white man's school in San Diego. He had learned the English language well but he had not forgotten his Navajo. He could read and write in Navajo and in English, and he had not been ashamed of it. Quiet Boy wondered what his father, if he were there now, would say of Black Chiddi.

"Go to school," said the letters from overseas. "Learn all you can about the white man's way. You will not regret it." Nespah had the letters yet, yellowed, but the writing was clear and bold. At first Nespah read them to him but now he could read them alone. Some of the words he could not understand yet, but enough. And in the box among the letters was the Purple Heart.

He could remember Ditsa Toddy only vaguely, such things as riding before him in the saddle as they tended the sheep, and the silversmith work. His father had been the best silversmith in Navajo Land. Everyone said so. Ti-wi knew it, and Atchee, though Atchee had not been born then. He had never seen his father. Quiet Boy felt pity in his heart for his younger brother.

Then they were there. They were on the high mesa. "This is it," Quiet Boy told them. "This is the place."

Yes, this was the place but there were not many nuts on the trees or on the ground. Someone had been there before them. Quiet Boy's heart fell. There would be no radio, no witch box. Well, that would please Grandfather. Of course, Grandfather did not know that Quiet Boy had planned to buy the radio with the piñon-nut money.

He should have gotten up before dawn instead of at sunrise. Still, there were a few nuts left in the trees and a few on the ground. These would be hard to find in the thick bed of piñon needles. However, the nuts had ripened early and were full, without blight or insect bite. The pack rats would not have had time to take many of them to their burrows for the winter.

Quickly, Quiet Boy and his family unloaded the harvest equipment from the wagon. Quiet Boy and Atchee thrashed the trees with long sticks, catching the few remaining nuts in a blanket to be separated later. What fun it was to watch the tiny nuts rain down on the blanket. Even Gogo danced and yapped. Nespah and Ti-wi raked the ground, and put the litter of nuts and cones and needles through a screen. The hardest work of all was the hunching of oneself along the ground, picking up the small nuts by hand.

It was late evening when Quiet Boy and Atchee with Gogo took a lard bucket and went looking for pack-rat burrows. They were poking in holes and scooping out nuts by the handful, when the quiet of the place was broken by the approach of horse's hoofs. It was Tall Boy. He carried a long nut-thrashing stick in his hand.

"Hello, sheep's tail." Tall Boy laughed. "Do you come so late you have to rob the pack-rat nests?"

Anger flowed through Quiet Boy, but he did not answer. He went on gathering nuts for the pail that Atchee carried. Someday he would lose his temper. He would fight Tall Boy, though he himself was much smaller. He would probably get the worst of it, but he would stand up to him.

"Hold your tongue," Grandfather had said. "It is better not to use force. The hour will come." Quiet Boy refused to look up or to answer Tall Boy's taunts.

"What do you think of Black Chiddi's stories at the Trading Post? Is he not right about the lessons? Is it not foolish to go to school? Do you not remember the movies and the books?"

Quiet Boy lowered his head. He looked at his younger brother out of the corner of his eye. Shame filled his heart. He remembered the movies. Some of them were bad for the Indians. They made the Navajos feel low, inferior and beaten.

Suddenly he heard a clatter of hoofs, a squeak of saddle leather, and looked around just in time to see Tall Boy and his pony dash toward Gogo. Gogo was smelling in a gopher hole and the horse and rider were upon him before he could escape. The horse reared and snorted, trying to miss the dog. Gogo scampered away just in time to miss the hard sharp hoofs, but not in time to miss the long stick across his right hip. It whacked, and the dog howled in pain and limped toward the underbrush. Away galloped Tall Boy, bursting his sides with laughter.

"See you at school," he shouted sarcastically and dashed out of sight.

Quiet Boy and Atchee lost no time in getting to Gogo.

"Come, Gogo," Quiet Boy coaxed, dragging the dog carefully from the bushes.

"Will he die?" Atchee wanted to know.

"I do not know," Quiet Boy said, wondering if the dog were hurt badly. Would there be a Medicine Sing to drive the Chindi, the evil spirit, from the dog's body? There were Sings for the people—the Dineh—and sometimes for sheep, but he did not know about sheep dogs. A tear splashed on the dog's head as the boy carried him in his arms to the green-covered wagon.

3: *Dancing Eyes*

WHEN NIGHT came, Quiet Boy and Atchee built a camp-fire in a clearing of the piñon-pine trees where Nespah and Ti-wi roasted the rabbit over the live coals. It tasted good eaten with the thin corncakes baked on the hot rocks.

"*Ahalani!*" Many Goats greeted them as he led his family into the firelight that night.

"That is good," Nespah told him, and they made room for the family of Many Goats.

Quiet Boy arranged some cedar wood on the campfire, and looked at Doli who stood with her head bowed in shyness. After a long time she peered up at him without raising her head. Soon they were all munching roasted nuts and talking in good Navajo fashion.

"I gathered three flour sacks full of the piñon nuts today," Pepe told them proudly.

That was more than Quiet Boy and his younger brother had gathered in all.

"And I, one and a half," Doli said quietly.

"And you?" asked one of the others.

"Two," Quiet Boy said, his heart sinking. Sheep's tail, he thought, and even then Atchee had helped him. If only Tall Boy had not interrupted!

"It was that others had come first," Ti-wi tried to explain.

"And Gogo," Atchee said, pointing to the dog curled up by the fire.

"And why Gogo?" Pepe laughed. "Did Gogo gather nuts also?"

"Gogo was hurt." And Quiet Boy told them the story of the boy and the horse and the dog, holding back all he could. Many Goats might think he had provoked the trouble.

"Let me see." The man knelt beside the dog and put knowing hands on his head, running them gently along his body and down his hind legs. Gogo winced a little, but he did not whine or offer to bite.

"He is not badly hurt. He will be all right soon," Many Goats advised them.

"It is bad for a Navajo to strike a dumb animal," Nespah said, shaking her head.

"Especially a sheep dog or a pony," added Yellow Corn, the wife of Many Goats.

"Tall Boy rides with Black Chiddi too much these days," Many Goats said. "The man is plainly a trouble-maker."

The little group sat silently staring into the fire for a

few minutes. A Navajo did not usually make trouble in his own group.

"Hide-and-Seek!" Atchee called out, and soon the piñon trees seemed full of dark little figures darting here and there, while the hills rang out with their shouts and laughter. Quiet Boy forgot for a time that he was the man of his mother's hogan.

Once he slipped away in the bushes and stalked the others as they played, just as his father had probably stalked the enemy. He hid in the sandrock cliff far from their campfire, and sat looking over the campfires of the other nut gatherers. How brightly the fires burned, scattered here and there among the trees and hills and along the mesa top!

They reminded him of the great Indian Ceremonial Campground at Gallup that his father had once taken him to see. He had been only five then but he remembered a little, and Nespah and Grandfather had told him much more. There had been hundreds of wagons, pickup trucks and cars from all over the United States. They had come from Iowa, Wisconsin, New York, the Dakotas, Washington, and Oklahoma and many other places. He hadn't known there were so many Indians in the world, let alone all the other people. The tribal dances were beautiful and he knew many of them himself. He knew, too, that many secret, sacred parts had been left out of the public spectacles. These parts were performed

only upon serious occasions and among their own people.

But the races had been the most fun of all. How Quiet
Boy loved a pony race. In his mind's eye he could see
the horses now, stretched out along the circle of race
track, and hear the shouts and whoops of laughter. He
remembered the booths with the pretty colored flags flying in the breeze.

Quiet Boy rose and stretched wide his arms. Surely
nothing could be more beautiful with the light of the
bright campfires scattered over the hills and mesas
against the backdrop of the night. He loved his Navajo
Land, its people, its schools, and its special events. No
matter what Black Chiddi and Tall Boy said, he wanted
it all. Why couldn't everyone, the Indian and the white
man, follow the same trail? Why must it be one or the
other? But he must go back to the wagon now before
they missed him. Already the shouts of the others had
quieted.

"Tell us a story before you go," Ti-wi cried, when the
family of Many Goats made ready to leave for their own
wagon camp.

"Yes, a story!" all the young ones shouted.

"A story about the Navajo Marines," Quiet Boy
pleaded.

Many Goats sat down again, adjusted his stump of a
leg, and began.

"The Navajos could crawl through the jungle without making a sound. They could take cover behind bushes their comrades had hardly noticed were there. They had no trouble getting around at night, for they were used to the desert darkness instead of lighted streets. Our commander said about us once, 'The only Indian who can't find his way back to his own lines is a dead Indian.'"

Everyone laughed at the joke.

"One more, please!" the young ones cried when Many Goats made motions to go.

"As you know," he continued, "Navajos have always been good runners. We have raced with the Zunis over a course twenty miles long. Well, in the battle areas, where there were no telephone lines, Navajos were called on to run with messages to the front. It was very funny when one of them was captured by his own side. The American boys would see the brown skin and dark eyes and be sure they had caught a Japanese disguised in an American uniform. Once a man rushed into camp and said, 'Got to report, I heard two Japanese talking on our line today!' A Navajo grinned and said, 'Oh, that was just us boys!'"

That was the best story of all. Quiet Boy wondered if his father had said that. He thought about this for a long time that night as he lay on his sheepskin, covered with his mother's good warm blankets. The nights were frosty in the high country in late October. Yes, Manwind and snow would surely come soon.

But it was hot as they drove through the desert valley toward home next day. It seemed strange that it could be so cold at night and so warm the very next day. But that was the way it was in Navajo Land. Even the ponies were too drowsy to be much disturbed when a covey of blue quail flew up from under their noses and scattered over the prairie. Doves sat quietly on the greasewood bushes and watched as they passed near by. Rabbits rested in their warrens, eyes half closed, and a chaparral cock ran down the road close in front of the green-covered wagon. This road runner was thought to be a good omen.

They came upon the wagon of Many Goats halted in the shade of a cottonwood tree that grew on the bank of a little wash or creek. Only Doli was at the wagon. She was weeping bitterly.

"It is my little sister, Dancing Eyes," she told them between sobs. "She is lost, gone," and she gestured with her hands over the countryside. "After we had eaten, it was so hot we slept a little. When we awoke Dancing Eyes was not here, and she has only twenty months, as yet."

"Let us look quickly," Nespah said.

"But where?" Ti-wi cried.

"Everywhere there is a place to hide." Doli spoke through a fresh burst of tears.

And Quiet Boy knew it to be so. There were clumps of sagebrush and rabbit brush, and hollow places in the earth. There were small ledges of sandrock, greasewood bushes, sand dunes and globed plants without number.

"Where are the ponies?" Atchee asked.

"My father and Pepe have gone on them to search in the valley and down the gully wash. My mother is over the rise while the young ones are gone on ahead, searching for the precious one."

Quiet Boy's heart ached for this girl.

"Then I will go up the gully wash," he told her. "The rest of you keep searching the sagebrush and every clump of saltweed near here."

"Dancing Eyes! Dancing Eyes!" they called. "Come, little one. Come quickly!" But only the sound of their own voices broke the noonday stillness.

As fast as his legs could carry him Quiet Boy ran, looking far before him, leaving the close-by places for the others to search. When he finally stopped to catch his breath, to wipe the perspiration from his eyes, he searched the area around him. It was very hot. The baby might die in the heat, not knowing enough to take shelter in the shade of the scrub, as an animal's instincts told it to do. Still—she might be hidden there, sleeping. Quiet

Boy peered into the bushes. He stopped to look here into a coyote den, there a badger hole. He looked for tracks in the soft earth and saw only the imprints of the little earth people. Small trails were made by the lizard and the horned toad, the snake, and others like them. The trail of a field mouse crossed the smooth sand in the gully wash. But there was no trace of a little lost girl.

"Dancing Eyes" he called, as he ran on and turned his head to listen for a baby answer. Once he saw a white-striped skunk family crossing the sheep trail in front of him. "One, two, three, four, five," he counted as he ran on.

An antelope bounded from a clump of bushes in front of him, then another and another. The third one was an albino, as white as a newborn lamb. What a rare thing! If he were not searching for a small child, he would trail and watch them further. When he hunted again, he would remember this place. An all-white antelope skin would bring much money. Such an animal was larger as a rule, heavier, and the fur or hair thicker. Quiet Boy knew that only once in many seasons would there be born a white deer, an antelope or an albino bear, a stripeless black skunk, or a black fox.

And because those animals were different their families did not understand and were uneasy. The odd ones were usually driven away, for their coats did not blend with the desert. They would be easy prey to larger animals or man. But the gods had also made them wiser, more cunning than most, and they grew larger and healthier. That is why they were more valuable.

He stopped short. Some wilted verbena flowers lay on a wide bare sandrock in the bottom of the wash! No animal would pick flowers and drop them there or anywhere!

"Dancing Eyes!" he called, cupping his hands around his mouth to make the sound carry. Again and again he called.

"Aaa," finally came an answer not unlike the sound of a small lamb.

Quiet Boy stopped and listened.

"Aaa," came the sound again and finally he saw her.

High on a sandrock cliff she sat, facing the wash, the breeze blowing her black hair. Quiet Boy quickly climbed the banks of the wash to reach her.

"Aaa," she said as he came near, "see," pointing down into the gully wash. Quiet Boy went quickly to her, in one little hand she still held a few straggling verbenas and some evening primroses.

Then Quiet Boy caught the sound. It was a screaming, chattering noise. Peering over, he saw the cause of the commotion. A couple of chaparrals or road runners seemed to be doing a Fire Dance on a large flat sandstone in the wide wash from which he had come. No wonder the baby was fascinated! He, too, forgot that others were worried as he knelt beside her and watched.

While one bird fluttered its wings, chattered and danced, the other one darted here and there to bring sharp pieces of cactus to lay on the rock. Already there

was a half circle of the deadly spines. The performance reminded Quiet Boy of the tribal dances of his people.

As he watched, a long slim shape reached out of the tall grass that grew in a crack at the center of the sand-rock. It struck out at the dancing birds and drew back.

A snake! A deadly rattlesnake! The birds were hemming it in with the sharp stiff cactus plants, making confusion for him.

When the snake thrust out to strike again, his heavy body plopped down on a fishhook cactus. Quiet Boy knew how like a real fishhook or a porcupine quill it was. It could not be pulled out without tearing away the flesh.

The birds took turns resting, darting back and forth for more cacti, and doing the Fire Dance.

Suddenly as one danced and charmed the snake, the other darted in from the back to strike at the snake's raised head. The snake went down. Swoop! And he went down a second time, but he was up again rattling as if for life.

Swoop! Another peck on the head and he was dodging again. The birds chattered and danced and darted while the deadly rattler became more and more dazed and confused. Several cacti were now clinging to its body.

The road runners were attacking faster and faster. Like a flash one darted toward snake's coiled tail. The snake turned back and struck out but the bird was gone. His poisoned fangs struck deep into his own flesh. Quickly he let go and struck out at one of the birds again and missed. He went down into the mass of cacti and began writhing in agony. Finally he turned on his back and quieted down, his white belly gleaming in the hot sun. Quiet Boy was awed at the quickness of the snake's venom to kill.

The birds stopped the dance, shook out their feathers, chattered together for a few moments, then darted into the high grass and were gone.

Quiet Boy sighed with relief.

"Stay here," he cautioned the baby and went below. With a long stick he turned the snake over to examine its head. One eye was a black-reddish mass, the other was only a black hole pecked out by the birds. What strategy the birds had used to conquer their mortal enemy. They seemed half human.

"I'll bet there is a nest of baby chaparral close by," he told the little girl back on the cliff.

"Aaa," the baby cooed, and smiled up at him as he lifted her to his shoulder and started back to the wagons.

4: *To Santa Fe*

"COME, GOGO, boy! We must bring the sheep in for Nespah," Quiet Boy called when they finally reached the home hogan.

Still limping, Gogo obeyed. This little brown-and-white dog was the best sheepherder the boy had ever known. He saved the family many steps. He saved the lambs from coyotes, and possibly the sheep and the family from many a rattlesnake. How Quiet Boy had missed him only today in the search for Dancing Eyes!

"Yap, yap!" barked the dog, bringing in an old ewe which was slow and which wanted, to nibble one more bite of the green-brown October grass before being shut in for the night. If it were not for Gogo, Quiet Boy would not be able to attend the school. He would most surely have to stay with the sheep. Perhaps he should anyway.

"Come, Little Runt," he called to a young kid born out of season. Being feeble, for a long time it had been fed on a bottle with a nipple as the agent had shown them how to do. Now it was large enough to follow the herd and nibble at grass and leaves. A piece of blue yarn from Nespah's weaving was around its curly neck.

"A blue ribbon," Ti-wi had said, "like the ribbons on the animals at the Fair."

"He is pretty enough to win a blue ribbon," Nespah agreed.

Little Runt turned and gave Quiet Boy a playful butt with his curly head as the boy pushed and backed him into the corral and closed the gate.

Quiet Boy did not want to go back to school on the day after the piñon-nut hunt. It wasn't only that he didn't care to meet Tall Boy again, it was also because of what he had seen in the valley along the gully wash. He would like to set his traps there. He was sure he could catch a skunk, and perhaps a coyote or even—but of course he couldn't catch an antelope or a deer with a trap. Still, deer and antelope hunting season would soon be coming. Would Many Goats lend him his rifle? He thought about this for a while. He wasn't sure he wanted to kill a deer or an antelope, that is, unless it was needed badly for food.

But he would like to track the albino antelope, stalk and watch him. He could never get enough of watching the small earth people, the wildlife.

He liked school, of course. He did not believe what Tall Boy or Black Chiddi said about the unfairness of the white man—not really. Still, it must be true about the sheep raising. The Navajos had raised sheep for hundreds of years. They knew how to tend them. Who else could do it so well? Surely not the teacher nor the bookmaker. And there was the blanket weaving. The white man himself agreed that no one could weave a better blanket than a Navajo. Then there were the movies. They were exciting. He marveled at the pictures that flashed across the screen. It was like magic. The white man had great knowledge and skills. But why did the Indians always get the worst end of the deal on the screen? Why were they shown almost always to be in the wrong? What they saw was not exactly like the stories handed down by the Ancient Ones of his tribe.

But his mother would never consent to his leaving the school. He was sure of that. The thought of the package of yellowed letters flashed across his mind.

"I will go to Santa Fe!" he said aloud.

Nespah could not object to that. There was a man there they knew who wanted to train Navajo boys to make silver-and-turquoise jewelry. He would be paid well and go to school, too. He would send money home to the hogan. When winter came they would be needing money for warm clothes, for corn meal, beans, canned peaches, sugar, and many more things that Nespah would have to buy at the Trading Post. And the wool of the sheep would not bring enough money.

"This year the price of wool is going down," he had

heard an Indian at the Trading Post say. "There is a slump in the market."

Yes, he would have to earn money some way to help support his family. And that was good. He was, after all, almost a man now. As soon as the sheep were all safe in the corral and every chore done for the night, he would remind Nespah of the man in Santa Fe.

When his work was done, Quiet Boy sat at his father's old workbench. It was a large section of the trunk of a juniper, with scars and chipped places caused by many hammers and chisels. On its crude top many hands had worked at the silver jewelry. Hard work and beauty had gone out from this old tree trunk.

Quiet Boy needed practice badly, so he sat there and looked at things for a while. It had been a long time since he had made a concho belt or a bracelet. There were such short periods to work on jewelry in the school what with English and arithmetic, geography and health, and the many other subjects besides.

Nespah and Ti-wi were singing as they put away the supper dishes in the apple-box cabinets. Atchee whittled a slingshot, like the one Jack, the trader's nephew, had shown him at the Trading Post. Grandfather already lay huddled in his warm bed, very likely sound asleep. All was quiet and peaceful in the hogan. That is, all was peaceful except the thoughts running through Quiet

Boy's mind and the dread, the fear, that burned within his heart.

"I'm not going to the government school again," he blurted out. His words in Navajo rang through the hogan.

Everyone stopped. Atchee poised his sharp knife in midair as he looked up from whittling. Grandfather turned over in bed.

Nespah sat down on a low wooden bench covered with woolly sheepskins. She folded her hands quietly, and, though she looked troubled, she waited for Quiet Boy to explain. Ti-wi folded her hands in the lap of her long full skirt and waited, too.

"But, my son, why are you not going to school? What is wrong?" Nespah finally asked.

Quiet Boy avoided her eyes. He tried to explain about Santa Fe. When he had finished, Nespah remained quiet in deep thought.

Grandfather raised himself on a gaunt and trembling elbow.

"But, my grandson, why do you really want to go? You do not tell all. If my mind does not trick me, you have other reasons."

Quiet Boy was silent.

"When winter comes," Ti-wi said softly, "My mother and I cannot take care of the sheep, hunt food, weave blankets, cook for Grandfather and Atchee and—How shall these things be done, and you not here two days of each week to help?"

"Yes," Atchee added. "Who will help me set the big traps for the skunk and the coyote?"

"Man-wind and snow come soon," Grandfather sighed, "and I am stiff and my legs are slow." He shook his white head and lay down again.

"It is not the money we will be needing," Nespah said quietly. "As you know your father was a soldier, a Marine. The fifty dollars comes regularly from the government for his widow, and ten dollars for the first child, and five dollars for the others. Seventy dollars is money enough with the fifty sheep allotted us also. The increase of the sheep is for us. It is up to us to keep them well, to see that they do increase."

"Also to read the books and to learn many things," Ti-wi added.

Quiet Boy looked up at the new school dresses for Ti-wi hanging from the ceiling poles of the hogan. How good the new print smelled! It filled the hogan with its newness. He looked at the new shoes under the bed. They were real shoes—not moccasins. They were going-to-school shoes for his younger sister.

Then there were the new jeans and leather jacket for Atchee. Though he was eight years old, he had never gone to school before. What a great event that would be for him! Quiet Boy had been anxious to tell his younger brother all the things that he should know about his first days in school. What a thrill it would be to show him around the buildings, to take him to his own room, to meet his teacher. He would show Atchee the cafeteria and how to manage the new kind of eating equipment. What fun they would have learning to use the drinking fountain!

Quiet Boy felt hot with shame. His younger sister, Ti-wi, and Atchee, his little brother, had remained at the hogan to help with the sheep until they could be sold, perhaps in late October or November, and to help with the weaving so that he could go to school and not miss a day. They could all go to school after the sheep were sold. But he, Quiet Boy, came first. What a great responsibility had been theirs and they were uncomplaining. Now he had the school, the soft hands—and he talked of going away, of leaving them. He was acting like a coyote, and he knew that a coyote was the worst thing an Indian could be called. He was a coward.

Anger flowed through him because of Tall Boy, yes, and because of himself. He felt shame creep through him like the chill of Man-wind. Let Tall Boy quarrel with him if he must. He, Quiet Boy, would fight back. "It is better not to fight with force of blows," Grandfather had said. But "what is, is," he had also said again. It seemed there were some things that couldn't be avoided. They had to be done.

He did not look up but he could hear Nespah rummaging in the box of old papers and records. Without a word she placed the yellowing pages before him on the workbench. They boy glanced at them and got up. He knew what they contained. He had read them over and over. He thrust his hands deep into his pockets. The black agate was still there. Perhaps it didn't exactly contain magic, but it was a symbol, a symbol of trueness and skill. He began taking off his shoes to go to bed.

5: *The Black Agate*

THE NEXT morning Quiet Boy was at the Trading Post in plenty of time. But once there he dawdled aimlessly, waiting until everyone else was on the big yellow bus. He was deliberately the sheep's tail this time.

"Why do you always hold back?" Pepe asked him later, when he had traded seats with another boy in order to sit by his friend.

Quiet Boy didn't want to say at first. He didn't like Pepe to think he was afraid of Tall Boy or anyone else for that matter.

"The ones who get on first must sit in the back." He tried to explain it this way.

"You want to sit near that—that big man—the driver?" Pepe asked.

"Not—not exactly," Quiet Boy answered. Then his eyes blazed with anger. "Look! See, I am not afraid of Tall Boy! It is just that a good Navajo does not wish to fight—unless he should."

"Yes, I know," Pepe agreed. "Yet some Navajos are mean."

45

"Yes, mean," Quiet Boy said. "But someday he will learn. Tall Boy is smart." He could hear Tall Boy's laughter and loud talk in the back of the bus.

"I am going to win the marble tournament today," he was saying for all to hear.

"I had forgotten the tournament," Pepe whispered. When his friend didn't say anything he asked, "Will you play against him?"

Quiet Boy thought for a moment. He weighed the odds. A vision of the big silver cup that was first prize flashed through his mind. How wonderful it would look on the workbench among his father's silversmith tools! And that wasn't all. The winner of the school championship would go to Winslow to play in the district tournament.

"I will play," he said.

"But if you win—"

"If I win," Quiet Boy answered, "I may have to fight."

The bus was at the school then, slowing to a stop. Quiet Boy got up quickly and stood by the door. Pepe followed him. As soon as the door opened they slipped off the bus and ran across to the marble grounds. There was plenty of time to limber up stiff fingers before the bell rang. The tournament was after lunch, but that gave only a fifteen-minute recess and a short noon period— not much time to get ready.

Quiet Boy spent every minute he could playing marbles. He played everyone in the school except Tall Boy. Tall Boy, they said, was the champ. He carried three tobacco sacks of marbles besides his pockets full. He had won over everyone except Quiet Boy. More important, he was the winner of last year's tournament. It was whispered that he hadn't won it fairly. But he had won. The silver cup had been his for a whole year.

When lunch was over and the last lessons in English and geography were done, everyone gathered around the tournament circle. Mr. Marshall, the new principal and tournament judge, placed thirteen marbles in the center.

"Now this is the way the game goes," he explained to all who were listening. "You are to knock the marbles out of the circle. Your taw, your shooter, must stay inside the circle. If it goes out, your turn is over. The one who knocks out the most marbles wins the game. The boy who wins the first two games out of three wins the championship."

Yells went up in Navajo and in English. Excitement was growing. Even many of the teachers stood watching. This was a great day for the school. Quiet Boy looked at Miss Burns as she held the trophy. He had always liked his teachers, especially Miss Burns. She smiled at him. Quiet Boy was proud to be in the game, frightened a little, yes, but proud.

"Last year's champion starts the game," Mr. Marshall told them. "They tell me it was Tall Boy."

And Tall Boy bent down on one knee for the first shot. His yellow taw drove one marble out of the circle. His second shot went wild. It was Quiet Boy's turn.

Quiet Boy aimed carefully. As he was about to let go of the black-agate taw, Tall Boy, standing near, blew his nose loudly. He jumped and the agate shot wide of its mark.

Quiet Boy was not sure but he felt that the nose blowing was done deliberately to make him miss.

Tall Boy led out in his next turn, knocking three marbles out of the circle. Quiet Boy also knock out three his next turn but he was behind. Tall Boy soon knocked out the remaining marbles to win the game.

"I am still the champ," he shouted, making a double fist handshake above his head. "Might as well quit." He nudged Quiet Boy. "I go to the district again this year."

When the boys lined up for the third game, Quiet Boy felt steadier, yet the other boy was out in front with the first game won and a tie with him in the second. Soon they had three marbles apiece.

Each of the three other players had one. Tall Boy missed the next shot by a hair's breadth. Quiet Boy's black agate smashed into the center marble knocking two out of the circle. The crowd cheered as Quiet Boy won the third game five to four.

"Tall Boy Yazzy and Quiet Boy Toddy will battle for the championship in the next game," Mr. Marshall an-

nounced. "The other boys will play for third and fourth places later."

Someone flipped a coin that gave Tall Boy first shot, and the tense crowd moved in closer.

Tall Boy's first shot was a whiz. It burst into the center pot and knocked out two marbles. He won another marble in the next shot. Then he missed.

Down on one knee, Quiet Boy aimed steadily. Just as his thumb flipped out the agate, a loud snort burst in his ear. It was Tall Boy blowing his nose again. Quiet Boy winced and the agate missed its mark.

lessly waiting. Out of the corner of his eye he saw Tall Boy step up close beside him, too close. The boy intended to play the same trick.

Quiet Boy hesitated, leaned forward to brush away a pebble and again took careful aim. He hesitated again, waiting for something—and there it was—a loud snort and his arm was jarred. But Quiet Boy smiled to himself and an instant later he shot. The marble smashed into the pot. A roar went up from the crowd as the marbles popped out of the circle and the black agate stopped just short of the inside line.

"Wow!" the crowd screamed. "Quiet Boy wins!"

When the noise quieted down, Mr. Marshall stepped forward and presented the silver cup.

"A good game," he smiled, "and good luck to you in the district tournament."

"*Ukehe,* thanks." Quiet Boy smiled weakly. He shot a glance at Tall Boy who was scowling from under his dark eye brows. And Chee, son of Ditsa Toddy, knew that the game—the real game—was not over.

6: *Little Runt*

THERE WAS always much to do at the hogan on week ends. Quiet Boy was glad of that. It was good to get away from Tall Boy and his friends for a while.

Quiet Boy noticed that the gang that followed the boy lately seemed to be growing. He didn't understand that. He had won the marble game fair and square. There had been plenty of witnesses. The judge was the principal.

"It is whispered that you cheated," Pepe had told him. "Tall Boy's friends are unhappy. They say you make trouble at school."

Quiet Boy's heart ached when he thought about this as he and Atchee rode the ponies, driving the sheep to the far grazing places on Saturday morning. Gogo limped along behind them. They had far to go today, for Quiet Boy would save the nearer grazing places for the others during the week while he was away at school. It bothered him, though, that Nespah and Grandfather had to take the sheep so far to the watering place. The windmill was three miles away. Still he was thankful

that the government men, or the "water witch" which-
ever the credit belonged to—had given them a well.
The gully wash was nearly always dry and the spring
had stopped flowing two years before. There had been
little rain this year. The grass was bare and brown. The
gods were surely angry now. Some said it was because
the Indians had taken up the white man's ways, the
ways of the *pelicani*. No doubt Black Chiddi had told
them this. And it was true that the *ye-bi-chai* had seem-
ingly done little good lately. Sometimes it did help and
sometimes it didn't.

Quiet Boy began to sing, for he was sad and unhappy.
He sang the song he had heard sung many times by his
people during the dry summer months.

> *"Send the rain to us*
> *Send the rain clouds*
> *Send the showers*

> *"You who walk in beauty*
> *You who walk the earth floor*
> *Send the dark mists."*

"Look!" Atchee pointed as he came galloping toward
his brother. High in the sky three soaring hawks
wheeled, making lazy circles. The giant birds were like
living gliders. Akin to the eagle they were, and with

almost as much magic. The boys watched as the hawks suddenly changed their flight and began to tease a flock of blackbirds, driving them like sheep before them, yet never attacking. Once a bird swooped low over Quiet Boy's head, and a feather floated downward.

"Ya hai!" the boys exclaimed, and pressing their heels to the ponies' sides they galloped to where the feather lay in the brown grass.

"It is a good omen," Quiet Boy said, tucking the feather into Atchee's headband. "It is yours. You saw the hawks first."

Near the gully wash they stopped to set the big traps they had brought, thrown across the backs of the ponies. They baited them with a fresh cottontail rabbit that Gogo had managed to catch. They watched a small sparrow hawk hovering above the ground. It was squealing loudly. When a field mouse popped out its head to see what the commotion was about, the sparrow hawk darted down, hooked his claws about its head and was gone.

"Ei yei! I wish I could fly like that!" Atchee cried.

"Someday I am going to fly," Quiet Boy told him. "I'm going to fly in a plane," he went on, knowing that every Navajo boy wished to fly. At the Fair, the Indian Ceremonial they would often spend their last dime for a ride.

"It is a witch bird, a devil spirit and bad medicine

for the people," Grandfather always said, so Quiet Boy had never flown.

"We must hurry. The sheep are going astray!" he cried now, and back to the little herd they galloped, kicking up a whirlpool of dust as they went, singing the Eagle song.

"E-e-ne-ya-e-a-ne-ye-na-ya
He-ye-ye-ye-ye."

"One, two, three, four—forty-eight, forty-nine." Quiet Boy counted and then stopped short. One of the flock was missing. "We were away for only a minute," he said.

"One, two," Athee began counting.

Many times a day they counted the sheep just to make sure. What could have happened? They looked everywhere. Had they made a mistake in counting this morning? The gate had been closed tight, and Gogo had not barked in the night.

"Yap, yap!" barked Gogo now far behind them.

"A-aa," went another sound, not unlike the one made by Dancing Eyes when she was lost.

"It's Little Runt. He is playing a joke." Quiet Boy laughed. "Why did we not think of the kid at first?"

"A-aa," cried Little Runt, darting here and there, jumping over bushes and climbing sandrock bluffs. The piece of blue yarn still around his curly neck was flying in the breeze.

"Blue," Quiet Boy said, "blue stands for gentleness and happiness." The color fitted Little Runt, he knew. He was full of tricks and right now was trying to confuse poor Gogo.

The late-to-be-born kid, with his tight white curls and very pink nose, was an interesting and lovable creature. Everyone loved Little Runt.

Soon they were near the tall shiny windmill.

"I smell the water!" Atchee cried, "and so do the sheep." He pointed.

And, sure enough, in the little flock, until now grazing slowly toward the mill, many heads were raised. The sheep sniffed the breeze coming from that direction, and began running forward.

"A-aa! A-aa," they cried as they ran. Only the very old ones, like Grandfather, measured their steps, bringing up the rear.

"Yes," Quiet Boy noted again and smiled, "a sheep's tail is always behind." And that was what the book had said, his old First Reader, about little Bo-peep and her sheep that wagged their tails behind them. He had liked that story, and the story about "The Boy Who Cried Wolf," and "The Little Black Sheep." He was glad that Atchee would soon read these. It did something for one to read. It helped him become a man.

They sat on their ponies at the big watering trough,
built by the government men, and watched the horses
take long gulps of the clear cool water. The animals'
large nostrils blew on the water surface, making funny
little rippled waves that grew and grew until they spread
to the edge. How good the water looked and good it
would feel trickling down thirsty throats!

"I would like to go swimming," Atchee cried.

"And I," Quiet Boy answered, "but not in the watering trough. It would not be good for the stock."

"Then how else?" Atchee wanted to know.

"There." His older brother pointed.

Soon they were off their ponies, stripped to the skin, shrieking and splashing under the cold stream flowing from the overflow pipe. They drank and they bathed. They ran and they splashed. They laughed and they screamed, playing a game of water tag. Never had the two brothers had more fun.

"It is too cold in late October!" Quiet Boy ran to the sunny side of the tank with his faded pants and checked shirt.

"This will be the last swim," Atchee said, his teeth chattering, lips blue from the chill.

"It is time to eat." They munched on sweet cakes from their mother's oven, which they had brought in their pockets.

"How good, after a swim," Atchee mumbled, his mouth full of the sweetness.

"Yes, good," his brother agreed.

They watched the birds fly in from far away. They saw them perch on the rim of the big tank and drink or dart down for a beakful and dart away again.

They looked at the many small animal tracks near by, even the coyote and the antelope tracks. Quiet Boy wondered if it were the albino antelope. How he would like to see him again, evil spirit or no!

"There is something you must see," and he told his younger brother about the encounter with the albino.

Beast, bird and boy seemed reluctant to leave the

watering place. But they all drank their last fill, and made ready to go. Grazing, the sheep went slowly back toward the hogan. It would be night when they reached there.

"The traps," Atchee reminded him, and Quiet Boy galloped up the wash.

It was up to him to make sure the traps were set correctly, while Atchee stayed with the sheep. They would not take another chance on losing one, not even Little Runt.

How tired they were when the sheep were finally shut in the corral that night! A warm supper was eaten, and the brothers stretched out in their soft sheepskins for a long time.

Quiet Boy awoke in the dark at the sound of Gogo barking. He opened one eye, and cocked an ear. He had slept so soundly and was still so tired that he was slow to pull his wits together. His mother and Ti-wi were getting up, also. Together they ran to the corral. There seemed to be a slight disturbance, a restlessness among the sheep. But they soon quieted.

"A coyote must be lurking about," Nespah ventured.

"Gogo can take care of a coyote, even with only three good legs," Ti-wi said.

"Yes," Quiet Boy agreed, "if there is only one coyote. But a coyote never fights fair. He will not attack alone."

Nespah examined the gate, and they all went back

to bed and finally to sleep. They slept the night through.

"One, two, three—forty-four, forty-nine—" Quiet Boy counted the sheep next morning before breakfast. One was missing!

"It is Little Runt," Ti-wi cried. "Little Runt is not here."

"Little Runt plays tricks." And Quiet Boy told her about the incident at the wash as they looked everywhere for the kid.

"There is not even a piece of bone, not even a curly hair of the kid left to be found," Atchee declared.

"Perhaps he got out of the corral some way, and wandered far, and the coyote caught him." Ti-wi's tears ran down her cheeks.

Atchee tried to soothe her. "We will get another pet."

"Never another like Little Runt," and Ti-wi buried her face in her hands.

Gogo followed them far and wide, poking his nose into gopher holes and bushes. Then he gave up. They found him curled up in his bed on the south side of the hogan in the sun.

"What's wrong, Gogo? Where is Little Runt?" Quiet Boy coaxed. But Gogo only wagged his tail and lay down again. "What is, is," he seemed to say.

Then Quiet Boy saw a strange thing. In Gogo's bed was a small piece of cloth, tan color and torn in the shape of the letter L. It was khaki cloth, like the slacks many of the boys wore. But neither Quiet Boy nor At-chee ever wore khaki. They wore jeans. Gogo sniffed the piece as the little family discussed it. "But who would want Little Runt? Why did they not take a fat sheep?" they asked one another.

Nespah only shook her head. It was a strange thing indeed.

At school Quiet Boy avoided Tall Boy for several days, even though the boy tried to appear more friendly toward him. He noticed that Tall Boy looked neater somehow. He realized why. Tall Boy wore his good clothes to school.

"Quiet Boy will report next," Miss Burns said one day in English class. And he went to the front of the room and began to read his report.

"In 1932 the Navajos had approx-approx-i-mate-ly" —Quiet Boy stammered on the big word—"576,000 sheep. In addition, they had 173,000 goats, each eating as much as a sheep. They had 21,000 cattle, and 44,000 horses, each eating five times as much grass as one sheep. If the food eaten by all these animals is added up, it is the same as if the Navajos had over a million sheep. That was more than twice as much as the reservation could feed."

Quiet Boy hesitated, the class was very quiet. He looked at Miss Burns.

"Go on." Miss Burns smiled. "It is an interesting report."

"There was only one so—solution. The Navajos must cut down on the number of sheep. They learned to care for a few and do it better with the help of the government and the CCC. Laboratories were built, schools and hospitals were established. Trucks were brought in and machinery and supplies. Dams and ditches were made, windmills put up. Better homes were built. The Navajo had a new way—a better way of life and they helped to make it so. The Tribal Council helped and still helps. But they are always in need of more members. Many Navajos are not interested in the new ways, in progress. Everyone who can should go to the Tribal Council meetings."

Quiet Boy stopped abruptly, folded his long report paper and started to his seat. Then it happened.

Tall Boy's long leg was stretched out down the aisle. It moved quickly as Quiet Boy approached. He saw the movement but he was too late. He stumbled and fell sprawling, hitting his head on the edge of a desk. There was a great commotion.

Tall Boy stood up, looking from Quiet Boy to the teacher. "I am sorry," he said innocently and pretended to help Quiet Boy up.

Already there was a large swelling above the left eye.

Tomorrow Quiet Boy's eye would be black and very likely closed.

"You must be more careful," Miss Burns said to Tall Boy as she dressed the wound, from which blood was oozing. It trickled down her patient's sleeve.

"I am sorry," Tall Boy said again. "No aim to do."

Quiet Boy felt dizzy, the pain racked his head, but what could he do when there was the apology, weak and half-hearted though it was? Still, there was one thing Quiet Boy knew. Tall Boy had taken Little Runt. Before he went down—when the leg shot out he saw it. A long L-shaped patch was newly sewed into the leg of Tall Boy's Khaki pants. Gogo had the other piece.

7: *Gogo*

IT WAS late in November and the winds were cold. The little hogan had a new door which was closed tightly at night to keep out the frosty air. Already several snows had come and gone. One light fall of snow came as soon or before the last one had melted away.

"It is strange weather indeed," Grandfather remarked. "Even Seventh Man, the great medicine man, cannot explain it."

"One, two—forty-one," Quiet Boy counted the sheep early next morning. Only forty-one sheep were left. The flock had been disappearing during the night, one or two at a time. This had been going on for the past several weeks. It seemed hopeless. Sometimes Gogo barked fiercely. He had done so only last night. "Whoever took the sheep took them before the snow fell," Quiet Boy told Nespah. "There are no tracks, not even a sign in the new fallen snow."

"If this keeps up, there will not be a lamb to report to the government," Nespah said sadly. "And us responsible—beholden for the ones we have." She talked a long time about their responsibility and troubles, about Black Chiddi and his tirades.

"Perhaps Mr. McClure, the agent, will come today," Quiet Boy said.

He wanted to talk to someone. He wanted to tell the agent about the sheep. It might be that the agent could help. But Mr. McClure did not come that day or the next or the next. And soon it was five days from Sunday, and still he had not come. Perhaps if they had a radio, as did many other Navajos, they could hear the news. They would know when the agent was to come or, if he didn't, why not. But Quiet Boy knew that Grandfather would never consent to a radio, a witch box, in the hogan.

"Bring an extra shirt on Monday," Mr. Marshall, the principal advised him. "That will be one day after Sunday," he added, knowing that the Navajos have a name for only one day in the week—Sunday. Other days are counted as so many days to or from Sunday.

Quiet Boy nodded and waited.

"Monday is the day for the district tournament in Winslow," Mr. Marshall explained.

"O'o, yes," Quiet Boy said in Navajo and quickly translated into English. "I had forgotten. But I cannot go." He looked disappointed.

"Cannot go? Why not?"

"It is the sheep," Quiet Boy explained. "Already ten have disappeared—gone." He gestured with his hands.

"You mean stolen? Did someone steal your sheep, too?" Mr. Marshall was concerned.

"Stolen I do not know," Quiet Boy said. "But gone, yes. Like that."

He put his hands in his pockets and shrugged his shoulders. He felt the agate. It seemed to have lost its magic, and the turquoise had, too, if it ever really had any. He glanced down at the wide concho belt. Of what good was a concho belt that held no magic? It did well to hold up his pants.

"Hmm," Mr. Marshall said. "Five people have reported the loss of sheep lately. Something must be done quickly."

"The government men—do they not know?" Quiet Boy asked.

The principal studied him for a moment. "Yes—yes, I think so," he said thoughtfully. "They seem to be working on it. But it takes time."

"Time, yes." Quiet Boy nodded.

"This is a large reservation," Mr. Marshall went on. "Sixty thousand Navajos, alone. Perhaps they will be along to hear your story soon, though. In the meantime, there is the tournament. Bring an extra shirt on Monday."

"But I cannot go," Quiet Boy told him. "There are

only forty sheep left, and no man in the hogan—only I. The little ones are there now, with my mother sick."

"That is bad," Mr. Marshall sympathized. "Very bad," he went on. "For if you do not go, then the boy in second place will be eligible—Tall Boy."

Quiet Boy winced. He hadn't thought of that. Still, he could not go. He had other plans. Let Tall Boy go then. That would be a part of his plans.

And Tall Boy went. He went to the tournament, and he brought home a trophy. How beautiful the gold cup looked in the trophy case at the school! Quiet Boy felt proud, knowing that he could have won, also, for hadn't he outplayed Tall Boy? He was proud because of one other thing—proud, yet sorry. Another sheep had disappeared while the boy was at the tournament. It couldn't be Tall Boy who was taking them away, at least not every time. Quiet Boy was glad he had not said anything.

When the agent finally came, Quiet Boy was with his sheep.

"I hear you are losing some sheep," Mr. McClure said when he drove up in his pickup truck.

"Ten," Quiet Boy told him.

"Wheee!" Mr. McClure whistled. "That is more than anyone else has lost. Have you a dog?"

"A good one," said Quiet Boy, pointing to Gogo who

was guarding the sheep. "The one the government man gave me."

Mr. McClure asked many questions. Did he go to school all week? Did he have brothers and sisters? How was his mother feeling? Did she have the flu? Did Quiet Boy go to the tournament? Who did? And then the agent went away.

The days grew colder and shorter in Navajo Land. It was December. To Quiet Boy the nights seemed dark and endless. He wrapped himself in sheepskins and sat out by the corral until late, guarding the sheep. One night his face was numb and his toes frostbitten when he finally came in.

"It is enough," Nespah said. "You will be sick. Let the sheep go. It is better to have loved ones than sheep."

And she helped him off with his clothes, putting hot stones wrapped in old rags to his frozen feet. She covered him with many woolen blankets. Quiet Boy did not realize how cold he was until he began to thaw out. How his toes ached and his nose itched! He did not go back to school for many days.

"I fear the flu," Nespah said to Ti-wi, looking anxiously toward the boy's bed.

"It is like winter of 1918, and again 1931," Grandfather grumbled in Navajo. He never tried to speak English. "Navajo is good enough for me," he always said. "The flu disease was bad then. The Dineh, the people, died of the sickness, and the sheep and horses froze in great numbers. Great Man-wind and snows come soon now."

The Ancient One was plainly worried, and he was right. He was nearly always right. He had seen many winters. The snow came and the wind with it. A strong north wind began to blow and big snowflakes settled down on the dry, bare earth.

But it was not Quiet Boy who first had the flu. It was Ti-wi.

"Frail she is and not going to school but a few days," Nespah moaned, making an herb tea and giving her *pelicani* medicine left over from the winter before. Ti-wi's eyes were bright, and fever racked her small body.

"Put my pretty dresses away," the little girl begged. Nespah took the newly made print things down from where they hung, from the roof logs and off the sewing machine. She folded them in the big chest. It would be a long time before Ti-wi could wear them to school again. Quiet Boy's own eyes filled when he saw Nespah's tear-stained cheeks. He laid his hand on Ti-wi's hot little forehead.

"Little sister," he whispered, but she did not answer.

Quiet Boy sat beside her bed far into the night. He sat there until Nespah rose to give her medicine.

"Will she get well?" he asked.

"I do not know," Nespah answered. "Perhaps we will have the Squaw Dance."

"Do we have the money to pay for the Medicine Sing?" Quiet Boy wanted to know.

"Grandfather will want it," she answered. "I have saved a little since the Night Chant for the Ancient One. If the mail runs—if the mail car can get through this blizzard—perhaps there will be the government check."

Quiet Boy felt better. They were doing all they could, all they knew how to do. Tomorrow he would mention

to Nespah about the *pelicani* doctor. He had heard about
the small magic pills and the shots, called penicillin. He
put a few more sticks on the fire in the center fireplace
then, and watched the smoke and sparks go through the
hole in the roof. How he wished his mother would consent to buying a stove, a *pelicani* stove! Many Navajos
now had them, some who were no more able to buy
than they. But he knew Nespah, always holding onto
the old things, the ancient customs. Now that they were
losing sheep, she would be firmer. And there was Grandfather. With the two of them, he and Ti-wi had had a
hard time bringing about much change. They were
lucky to have things like the sewing machine, the "gold"
bedstead with the fluffy mattress that father had bought,
and a real table with chairs. How he had wanted a radio,
but the Ancient One had refused. "The box is be-
witched," he cried whenever one was mentioned. The
Dineh did not contend with their elders. Even grown
men let the subject drop with Grandfather.

Quiet Boy slept as sound as a *pelicani* silver dollar.
When he awoke, everyone was up and outside. Everyone
except Ti-wi. She seemed to be sleeping peacefully in the
big bed. Quiet Boy found the corn-meal mush and the
"sweet salt," or sugar, which his mother had left by the
fire for him. He sat on the low stool covered with sheepskin and ate. How good the warm goats' milk tasted!
He felt its warmth all the way down.

When he went outside, he knew at once there was something wrong. "What is wrong? What has happened? Is another sheep missing?"

"A sheep, yes," Nespah told him. "But that is not all." She looked at him as if it were the end of the world.

"Gogo is dead," Atchee finally said and burst into tears.

"Ugh!" Grandfather snorted. "I think it is the *pelicani*. Who else?"

"No!" Quiet Boy was about to tell them whom he suspected, when Atchee pointed up the road.

"It is there," his little brother said.

Quiet Boy's legs fairly flew to the spot pointed out. Along the way he looked for tracks, for Navajos are the best trackers there are. They know the tracks of their own horses and many of their neighbors'. They can identify most of their acquaintances by their footprints. Quiet Boy knew that many criminals were caught and crimes solved by *pelicani* peace officers because they used Navajo trackers. But the snow flurry had again covered all sign.

"Poison," he said when they all came up to look at Gogo once more. "Someone has used poison meat. See the bone?"

And there it was only half eaten, a big juicy mutton bone, and the dog swollen and stiff.

Now they had no dog. The older Navajos liked to

have many dogs near their hogans. "They will keep away the evil spirits," some said. If this were true, Quiet Boy thought, then they themselves were doomed. There was no other dog, and they had been happy to get this one. A government man had brought him with the allotted sheep. "You need a good sheep dog," he had said. And there had been Gogo, a happy, bouncing mongrel puppy. He had been a good friend and good sheep dog. And for his loyalty he was no more.

"It is the government men, maybe so," Grandfather said as he hobbled up. "They put out poison for prairie dogs. They kill the coyotes and the pack rats, I heard at the Trading Post last summer."

"But that was long ago." Quiet Boy's heart was full of pain. "They would not put poisoned meat so close to the hogan in the dead of winter."

"Then who? Who do you say it is?" the Ancient One wanted to know.

"I cannot tell now, Grandfather. I do not know. But It is not the government men. Why should they give us sheep and then steal them? Why should they give us a good sheep dog and then poison him?"

Shaking his head, the Ancient One hobbled back to the hogan. He mumbled a prayer to the gods as he went. He took a small box from under his blankets and sprinkled a little corn meal along the trail. This, he believed, would keep evil spirits—the *chindi*—out of the hogan.

8: *Life or Death*

ATCHEE BROUGHT a piece of rope. Carefully they tied it to the dog's legs with a *chindee,* or granny knot, which is used when tying something to a corpse. They got on their ponies. The frozen ground was so hard the dragging left no marks.

It took a long time to reach the arroyo in the downwash where the great cracks in the rocks were, where Quiet Boy had seen the road runners battle the rattlesnake to the death. They were there at last. They coiled the rope carefully and lifted the body over the side. Slowly they let it down into the deep crevice. The boys were silent as they rode back to the hogan. It was an understanding silence, following them all the way.

"You must go back to school, my son," Nespah said, looking at Quiet Boy as he warmed his hands at the center fire.

"Ti-wi?" he questioned, seeing his little sister still sleeping.

"Sometimes better, sometimes not. At the moment the fever has left her."

"Then I shall go to school," the boy told her. "But if she grows worse, I can come home. I will return if you need me."

Ti-wi opened her eyes and smiled up at him. "You are a good brother," she said weakly. "I am hungry."

Nespah hurried to prepare mutton broth while the boys brought more sticks for the fire. They made a high stack of wood and roots by the door of the hogan so that it would be easy to reach if more snow came. Come it did, but not until Quiet Boy had gone back to school for the week.

"Winter is here," an old Indian at the Trading Post said, as the boy waited by the school bus. "The rattlesnakes are sleeping soundly. The ponies, I see, have put on their winter coats, and Man-wind blows strong today."

Quiet Boy's gaze went back over the road that led to the isolated hogan. He was forever being pulled in two directions.

By night everything was covered with a blanket of white. For five days and nights snow fell with a deadly stillness. Snow came up to the horses' bellies. It was heavy and full of water, and the evergreens at the school were weighted down with it. It was beautiful but frightening.

Quiet Boy, watching from his dormitory window, knew that it meant hardship for his people, the Dineh.

Some of the bough shelters for the stock would cave in under the weight of the snow. The stock could not find grass, not even the prickly pear, nor the yucca.

Only the tall cacti, the sagebrush, the juniper and piñon trees could be reached, and not even they if the snow continued. A horse could not go far in snow belly-deep, and it was already over the heads of the sheep. Gone was Quiet Boy's fear of the sheep being stolen. Now their safety depended on another matter. Not even a thief would go out in this weather.

Quiet Boy helped shovel paths through the snow to the classrooms. He watched the big snowplows go by clearing the highway, and he was troubled and anxious. If he could only hear from his family, his people! But there was no word from his hogan, no news of his little sister. He was glad that he and Atchee had hauled much wood and roots for the fire. He was glad hay was stacked in the shelter for the sheep and the horses. But who would feed them? There were paths to be dug to the corrals and the shelter.

It was true that Atchee was growing up, that he could do many things around the hogan, but he was still too young, at eight, for a man's work. He could not go for the medicine man or the *pelicani* doctor in this terrible weather.

"The snow is still falling and the wind is beginning to blow a gale," the radio report said on the fifth day as the boys and girls sat quietly in their classrooms and listened. Even Tall Boy sat silently for a time, his eyes on the *pelicani* witch box. A girl wept. Doli's face was gray with fear. Miss Burns looked anxious. Her eyes wandered over the group, lessons forgotten.

"I know you are all worried," Mr. Marshall said, coming into the classroom on Friday afternoon. "Perhaps the weather will change by morning. So, go on with the classes." He looked at Miss Burns. "It is better that way."

Then he went out, and Miss Burns took up a textbook, turning the radio low.

"Turn to page sixty-four," she said. "Read what you find there, then we will discuss it."

Quiet Boy turned to the page. He tried to read but his mind was elsewhere. There was not much food at the hogan. This was five days from Sunday, and Nespah always bought food for one week only. "It sometimes spoils," she said, "or weevils get in it."

His eyes tried to focus on the page. "New Mexico and Arizona were the last two states to join the union," he read, and could not go on.

"Stay off the highways," Quiet Boy could hear the faint voice of the radio announcer. "Stay in your hogans if possible. The government men will try to contact all isolated places. The snowdrifts are deep and dangerous. No school buses will run this week end. Snowplows will try to keep the main highways open. They will go to the out-of-the-way places as soon as possible. One more warning—stay off the highways—unless it is a life-and-death case!"

"Life-and-death case—life-and-death case," Quiet Boy said over and over in his mind.

"Class dismissed," Miss Burns announced and quickly everyone filed outside. There were a few shouts and snowball fights but not many. This blizzard was a solemn and dreadful thing. It was something that involved everyone in Navajo Land.

A little group gathered in the Big Room at the boys' dormitory and listened for news of the storm on the radio. What a useful thing the witch box was! Next year Quiet Boy would save his piñon money and buy one in spite of Grandfather's argument.

"Still snowing and blowing," the report said at intervals. "The snow is freezing and crusting over but still dangerous to walk through.

"Life and death—life and death," rang the other report in his ears.

The big clock over the mantel pointed to four. He was glad school had let out early.

He could be at the Trading Post by seven. The trader would keep him until morning. He was sure of that. Then he could borrow a horse to ride to the hogan, or even walk. Cutting straight across he could be there in three or four hours. He knew all the bluffs and canyons by heart; though they might be filled with snow, he could go around them. A horse had lots of sense, more than some gave him credit for. Instinct it was called.

Life and death—life and death—Ti-wi. "I'll come home if you need me," he had said to Nespah.

Up in his room he put on his warmest clothes, two pairs of jeans and two pairs of wool socks. He was glad he had his high top boots. He put on his wool knit sweater with the turtle neck, and his big sheepskin-lined coat. His cap with the ear flaps was also sheepskin lined, and the mittens that came in the mission Christmas box just recently.

Quiet Boy went out the back way and stepped onto the crusted snow. It had frozen almost solid in the last hour. By morning it might hold up the weight of a horse.

He looked up and down the highway. The falling snow had covered the black ribbon again, and the snow-plow was hardly out of sight. There was not a car to be seen. People must be heeding the radio warning. He would start walking slowly. Perhaps someone would pick him up before long. He walked along on the left side facing the traffic, if there had been any traffic. The book had said it was better that way, safer than on the side with cars coming from behind.

"Honk! Honk!" A car whizzed past him. The driver never even looked in his direction. Quiet Boy watched the car glide down the road. The back end wavered a little and tried to catch up with. the front. At first he thought it was going to skid or else land in the ditch. Then it seemed to right itself and went skimming onward again.

"The man should have chains," he said to himself. "Chains would clutch the ice and snow or the graveled road better." If he ever had a car of his own he would surely have chains for the snow.

Soon it was getting dark. It got dark early these January days. Already almost one month of the new year had gone, according to the little calendar on the wall of the hogan. He usually marked off the days with a pencil but things had been happening so fast lately, so fast!

Now it was days since he had left the hogan. He looked at the snow piled high beside the highway. The snowplow made a pretty thing, a good thing. The high piles helped him stay on the road. "Just stay between the rows of snow," he warned himself.

The fence posts were almost out of sight. They would be as soon as darkness came. Only the telephone poles were visible, that is, they were in the daylight. Fear gripped him when he thought of daylight going, and not a star to guide him, nor a mountain peak, nor anything. He stopped then and looked back, but not for long. The wind, Man-wind, which is the north wind, struck his face with a cutting blow. The snow, drier now and harder like sleet, pounded his back and beat against his legs.

He must walk faster to keep warm now,, for the last bit of daylight was going.

"Whir-r-r." Quiet Boy thought he heard a motor. He looked up and down the road but all was dark. If it was a car it was a long way off. If nothing came along to help, what would happen to him? He looked up, the snow sleet beating in his face, his neck stiff with cold. Thin black clouds scurried across a gray sky. Now and then, when the snow and wind let up, he could see a tiny star wink and disappear. There it was! He saw a moving light. An airplane was out in the storm. How he would like to be up there! It would be warm in the plane, close to a warm motor. He watched until it was gone.

Suddenly a great light spread out around him, a car was coming up from behind. He stepped to the side where the snow was piled and raised his hand for a ride. The car pulled up and stopped. The driver was waiting for him to get in. An Indian who sat beside the driver reached behind him and opened the back door. Quickly, as quickly as he could, Quiet Boy got in. He hadn't realized he was so stiff. He was like an old man, like Grandfather. He hadn't felt—

In the light that flashed on at the moment the door

opened he saw something—something that he did not wish to see.

The driver of the car was Black Chiddi.

"Where do you go, boy?" the man asked and Quiet Boy knew that Black Chiddi did not recognize him. That was good.

"To—to the Trading Post," he murmured weakly, partly because he was cold and partly because he was afraid.

Black Chiddi had no love for him, never had he liked him. Now that Quiet Boy knew why, he was more afraid than ever.

"Only last summer," his mother had told him recently, "Black Chiddi asked me about marriage."

Quiet Boy had been surprised, glad she had refused him, yet afraid. He had never told Nespah his suspicions. It was all because of evil spirits, Mother and Grandfather had agreed. The gods were angry because of this or that, they told each other. And all the time it had been Black Chiddi, an evil spirit, yes, a black devil spirit!

Quiet Boy beat one mittened hand into the other because of the cold, because of his anger at this one who called himself a man, and because of the plight he was in.

As soon as the car stopped at the Trading Post he would jump out and rush into the store before the driver had time to bring the car to a complete stop, before he found out who his passenger was.

Quiet Boy wriggled on the seat. He was warmer, it was true, but sleepy, very sleepy. If he could only lie down for a moment in the long back seat, and get a short nap, just a little one—Then he saw it in the flash of the dome light, when the man beside the driver looked at his watch, caught in a broken piece of the seat. It felt like yarn pressed against his cheek. There was a loop tied in it, a broken loop, about the size of Little Runt's neck. Were Tall Boy and Black Chiddi working together? He remembered the khaki patch.

Slowly he pulled the string loose from the seat and put it in his coat pocket. Tomorrow, when yellow dawn came, he would examine it closely. Right now he was sleepy—very sleepy.

9: *Trouble at Winslow*

QUIET BOY opened his eyes. It was very dark and cold and still. Where was he? Not in the dormitory, not in his mother's hogan, not at the Trading Post. Then he remembered. He was in a car, in the back seat of Black Chiddi's rusty car.

He tried to move but he could not. He was stiff with cold and numb all over. Slowly he moved one foot and then the other. He beat his hands together. If he had felt old like Grandfather last night, then he felt twice as old now. Finally, he could sit up and looked around. It had stopped snowing, wherever he was. Yellow dawn showed faintly in the east, that is, he supposed it was east. He could see the faint outline of buildings.

"I must move," he told himself. "I must get out. Black Chiddi may come back soon. He does his work in the nighttime."

Quietly he opened the car door, and got out cautiously. He must get away without being seen or heard.

He wandered around on the frozen snow in the dark for a while, staying behind the buildings. Yes, yellow dawn was coming slowly. Dark clouds still hung scattered in the sky, but the stars were going. The morning star was the brightest. It was his guiding star. Many times it had led him home to his mother's hogan. And he thought about that as he tramped on the hard crusty snow.

Nespah and Grandfather and Ti-wi and Atchee, they would be in the hogan, in the deep warm sheepskins, and in the big bed. They wouldn't know where he was, that he was lost, and, not knowing, they would not worry.

"I must go to them," he whispered. "When the Sun-Carrier is up, I will find out where I am. Then I will go back. Some way I will go."

A wind stirred in the sleeping night. As at a sign the day awoke. There was the sun, peeping over the hills. Its long fingers stretched out across the big white world. It had been a long time since Quiet Boy had seen the sun, a long time. Suddenly it sprang up from the earth and hung there, cheering him, filling his face, his body, with its yellow goodness. "Yellow is the color of corn," Grandfather had said. "It is the color of the harvest, of ripeness. It is life-giving." Quiet Boy held out his hands toward the sun, and it warmed him.

"I am hungry," his body said, his stomach flat inside him. Then he felt in his pockets and found some food. Piñon nuts he found there, and sunflower seed, and they tasted good. He found some more in the lining of his coat where the pocket was torn. He found a couple of matches too, that he had carried a long time for an emergency. But he did not need them yet.

He heard roosters crowing and dogs barking. Motors hummed and people called out. He began walking again toward the sun, farther away from the rusty black car.

He read the signs over the shops, Mack's Barber Shop, Bob's Garage, Winslow's Restaurant—Winslow! He had wanted to come to Winslow for the marble tournament. Now he was there. Black Chiddi had taken him right by the Trading Post clear to Winslow, Arizona. How could he ever get back?

"Hmm-m-m!" The food smelled good in Winslow's Restaurant! He looked at the sweet cakes in the window for a long time. When he saw a woman watching him, he went on. If he could find a policeman he would ask him about the roads around the Trading Post, and how best to get there. That is a policeman's job, to help the people. That is what the book had said.

He remembered the story Grandfather always told, too. It was an old story about the Navajo law, before the time of the Long Walk from Fort Sumner.

"There were only law chieftains then and they were Peace Chiefs. There were bad men, too. There were young Indian men who were strong and were out for trouble," Grandfather had said. "To do each other harm, the one who had the most friends tackled the other party. They took something away from them or else just settled things by force. When a person stole, by our old law, he had to pay back according to the value of what he took. Sometimes they just fought it out instead."

"The Peace Chiefs would lecture," Grandfather had said, "and talk to the troublemakers until they cried or decided to reform. When they said they wouldn't do it any more, they would take an ember out of the fire, spit on it, and throw it out the smoke hole with the crime. "I am rid of my faults. I will never do it again," they would say. That is the way a Navajo reformed," Grandfather had told him. "That was the custom of us Navajos in the days when there were no police."

It was a long story and Grandfather would tell it all. He never tired of telling the old stories.

"But times have changed," the Ancient One had said, "Schools came to the Navajos and law enforcement also, with Navajo judges. Now it is an institution, and it is good, I think."

Quiet Boy knew his Grandfather was not like some of the Ancient Ones. He was never very bitter about the changes. He did not hate the white people, nor their laws, nor the policemen—not much.

"The policemen are here to protect the people," he told Quiet Boy. "They are like a powerful medicine man, like a powerful performer of ceremonies. They are like a *pelicani* doctor. Even though there is peril, a doctor goes in anyway. That's the way policemen are. No matter how hard their duties, they perform them."

And that's the way it was. Grandfather was right except about having a radio. Grandfather would never let him have one.

"Morning, son." A gruff voice spoke into Quiet Boy's right ear, and he jumped sideways.

"Don't be afraid," said the big policeman. "I want to help you."

Quiet Boy looked into his eyes then. He saw they were friendly and twinkled, and that their gaze was steady. Quiet Boy told him his story—all of it, even the part about Black Chiddi. The man listened and wrote in a little notebook. When he had finished he said, "Go down to that garage. See that sign?"

"I see it," the boy answered.

"Stay there until I come for you or send you word. It is warm in there."

Then the policeman left, and Quiet Boy went to the garage. It was warm inside where the men were working and talking.

He sat behind the stove that had a fat belly, fatter than his belly, and listened to the radio messages. Quiet Boy grew warm and sleepy, and as he sat hunched there he slept.

"The Indians are in grave danger," the voice on the radio blared out as Quiet Boy awoke. "Many Navajos in isolated places are snowed in, and have been for several days. Their stock is freezing and starving. It has been decided to step up the hay lift. Army and Navy planes are to drop hay for the stock and food for the people. As some of you remember, this was done successfully in the blizzard of 1931."

Quiet Boy had heard of that other time. Some of his relatives and friends had suffered terribly. Many had died of the lung sickness and the flu. He thought of Ti-wi and his heart was sick. They wouldn't be able to have even a little Sing for her now because of the blizzard. Neither the medicine man, nor the white man's doctor could get through to the hogan. But Nespah knew a few of the songs and chants. She didn't use them much anymore, but she would if there was no other way. Ti-wi would know they were trying. It was good just to know that someone cared.

Quiet Boy waited all day and the big policeman did not come as he had said he would. Neither did he send word. What could be the matter? Something must be wrong. "A policeman's tongue is straight," Grandfather had said. "One can trust the Peace Maker."

Still he did not come. The men who had been there to have work done began to go away. The owners of the garage were cleaning up and putting tools away. Quiet

Boy thought of his father's tools on the juniper work table at his mother's hogan. Then he slept again.

When Quiet Boy awoke, he saw a boy about his size looking at him, eating some candy that he had in a striped sack.

"You want some?" the boy asked, holding it out.

"Thanks," Quiet Boy took some of the candy eagerly, two pieces. It was good candy—jawbreakers. He popped a piece into his mouth. It would last a long time. The boys walked around on the street a while as they sucked on the candy and talked a little. They didn't have to talk much, they just seemed to understand each other. The boy's name was Douglas.

"You speak good English," Douglas said. "You would pass for one of us."

"You would make a good Indian," Quiet Boy told him, and they laughed together.

Quiet Boy told him about his home and his sister, about Black Chiddi and the policeman.

"It's in the paper and on the radio," Douglas said. "The policeman got shot! Do you think it was Black Chiddi who fired at him?"

"That I can't tell, but I know something was wrong when the policeman didn't come back, for he looked like a good man. Is he hurt bad?" Quiet Boy asked.

"He is in the hospital, shot in the leg. The bandit got away though, drove north and east on the highway."

"Toward Canyon de Chelly," Quiet Boy said half to himself. "That is Black Chiddi, no doubt."

"Do you think we should report where he might be going? There is a reward you know."

"Reward?" Quiet Boy pondered.

"Yes, a thousand dollars, dead or alive."

"Wheee! That's a lot of money. But he has to be a bad Indian, this one who shot a policeman. We would want to make sure it was Black Chiddi before we set men on his trail. There could be another one, a bandit, I mean."

"It might not be the same policeman, either," Douglas said, "but I'll bet it is. I must go home now. It's pretty late. Want to go with me? You could sleep there."

Quiet Boy hesitated. That sounded fine. "I had best go back to the garage and wait a little longer," he said finally. "I told the policeman I would wait there."

"I'll see you later then." Douglas waved as he hurried down the street.

"The Navajo Indians are having it rough," one of the men said as Quiet Boy came in again. The boy pricked up his ears. Every morsel of news was relished. The radio had been turned off.

"I don't know about that." The other one swept behind the stove. "They are tough and used to hardships like that. They are a little like animals, I think, not caring for the better things of life."

The first man glanced at the boy, then he spoke again.

"Some of them maybe, but not all. I know some good Indians. Now take that Harry Begay, who comes in here sometimes. He is a good Navajo, trying to make things better for his people. He's on the Tribal Council, and works with the government agencies. He's smart, too."

"But that's just one, one out of a thousand," the other man said, intent on his sweeping. "Not many are like that. Most of them are ignorant and don't care, probably can't learn."

"Could if they had a chance," the other went on. "Just like us, I say. Some try to learn and some don't. Some are good and some are bad, just like everybody else."

Quiet Boy went outside then to look around for the policeman again. But he didn't see him, and it was growing late. He walked for a long time on the streets and he didn't even see another officer.

He looked in a bakery window and thought he could smell the pretty cakes and loaves he saw there. Then he ate the other jawbreaker as he walked back to the garage. He passed by the place where the rusty black car had stopped, but it was gone.

"Some are good and some are bad," the man had said, and the man was right. Quiet Boy thought about this as he waited outside, for the doors were closed now and locked. A small night light was left burning in the back.

Everyone was gone off the streets, and it was growing darker and colder.

Quiet Boy adjusted his cap and fastened it under his chin. Then he put on his mittens, buttoned up his coat, and looked around carefully.

There were a few old cars parked near the place, most of them wrecks with the glass broken out. He selected the best one, a pickup truck with only one broken window, and climbed into it. He wished he had gone with Douglas.

It was going to be awfully cold tonight, colder than last night, the report said. He found a piece of cardboard and put it in the window, to cover the hole where the glass was broken out. There were some old gunny sacks on the floor of the pickup. He wrapped them around his feet and legs. There were not enough to cover his body as he lay down on the seat. He was warm enough now, and the seat was soft and comfortable. In the hogan he was used to sleeping on the floor with only a sheepskin under him.

But he couldn't sleep for a long time, so he thought about things—the things he had heard the two men say in the garage, people he knew like Douglas, who had offered him a warm bed, Mr. Marshall, the principal, and Miss Burns, his favorite teacher. He thought about the policeman he had talked to, and about Tall Boy and

Black Chiddi. Then he thought about people he had read of in books, like Kit Carson and Buffalo Bill, who were friendly toward the Indians, and Abraham Lincoln. Then he slept.

10: *The Hay Lift*

QUIET BOY slept fitfully, getting up several times to walk around, beating his fists together inside the mittens. The cold kept seeping in and finally he thought of the matches in the lining of his coat. The cardboard in the car window was dry and would light easily. He remembered the pine shavings and trash the men had swept out of the garage. If he could only feel his way to them in the dark! And he did. There was no moon but the starlight on the snow was enough when his eyes became adjusted. A plane buzzed low overhead.

Soon he had a small fire glowing there behind the garage, out of the wind, where the snow had been cleared away. He took off his mittens, and passed his hands back and forth through the warm smoke and thin blaze. He squatted there by the fire and warmed his mittens before putting them on again.

"What's going on here?" A voice spoke and Quiet Boy stood up abruptly.

"I—I was cold in the pickup." He gestured toward it,

in the firelight, thinking the man was an officer of the law, and hoping he was.

"You mean you slept in the pickup?" the man asked.

"For a while," the boy answered. "I—I'm just waiting here for a ride home to the hogan. I have a warm bed there and food, at least there was food when I left."

The man looked at him a moment, realizing he was only a boy. "Come into the house," he said, pointing to the back of one across the alley. "It's warm there, and we can talk."

Quiet Boy pointed to the fire. "It is dangerous to leave this burning alone," he said.

"I'll squash it," and the man began to push the sticks and trash aside with his heavy boots.

When they had trampled out the last spark and raked snow over the embers, they went inside. It was the warmest house Quiet Boy had ever known. He soon took off his coat and cap and put them on a chair.

"Put your feet in the oven," the man directed, opening the door to show him, "if that won't warm you up too quickly and make the bones ache. Here is some hot coffee.

"I am a construction worker at the airport," the man told him. "I live here alone, but I must go now. I must be at the airport at four-thirty this morning to move some equipment. Several planes are due there right away."

"May I go with you," Quiet Boy asked, "to the airport?" He had given up hope of seeing the policeman again.

"Might as well," the man said, after hearing his story. "They might take you back, drop you out with the hay and the food." He grinned.

When he had eaten the last piece of bacon and the last crumb of bread, Quiet Boy put on his coat and cap. He dreaded going out again, but it had to be done. "What is to be done, is to be done!" Nespah always said.

"Everything is being done for your people that can be done," the man told him, and Quiet Boy believed it. "The Red Cross, the Army, the Navy, the State Highway Department and many other organizations are answering the call."

Snowplows, tractors, jeeps, horses were working their way to the penned in people, and Quiet Boy's heart was grateful. Perhaps they would reach his own hogan in time.

"For several days food, hay, and firewood have been dropped near the hogans," the man told him as they rode.

There were many planes and people at the airport. There was a hustle and a bustle everywhere and Quiet Boy's head swam with the excitement of it.

How glad he was to see some Indians, Navajos like himself, gathered around the door of the hangar! When the construction worker let him out, he went to them at once.

"*Ahaloni!*" they greeted him, seeing he was a Navajo.

"Are you one of the men?" one of them asked him in Navajo. "Did the Tribal Council send you? Are you going on the plane?"

"I would like to go," Quiet Boy said quickly, yet not knowing what it was all about.

Then they told him the story. Yes, for several days food, hay, and firewood had been dropped near the hogans. But many hogans had been missed, passed by because the pilots and guides did not know the country well. They could not spot the places in that land of snow. They had maps and plots of the general location but there were isolated hogans. Quiet Boy knew that this was true. His own hogan was likely one of those passed by. Many Goats' and Tall Boy's hogans, would be hard to find too, and there were many others.

"We are asked to go as guides," the Navajo told him, "because we know our own land, our own hogans. We can show them where to drop food and fuel so that our people can get it, and not starve or freeze."

"But there are not enough of us Navajos here," one told him. "Perhaps you could go, too."

"I can go," the boy said. And they went to tell the government men, the pilots and the others.

"He is only a boy," one pilot said, looking him over.

"I am almost a man," Quiet Boy answered quickly. "I have thirteen years." And he did have. He had been twelve last year but now it was a new year. He hadn't had a birthday yet, but he would soon, which doesn't matter much to the Indians anyway. "It is what you can do that counts," they always say. The Navajo explained this now to the men, especially to the doubting pilot.

They were desperate for guides for some places, and it was time to take off, before the fog became too heavy.

"You are tall and responsible-looking for thirteen," the pilot said meditatively, and Quiet Boy pulled himself up even taller. "What is your name?"

"Chee, son of Ditsa Toddy," the boy said proudly. Indians do not use their real names often. There is an old idea that names have magic, and if said too often would use up the magic. "Quiet Boy is my nickname," he added.

"And your home?"

"Near the Canyon de Chelly. At the mouth of it, where it opens out into the desert. There are many smaller canyons and hills and gully washes near there where people live," he ran on, the words tumbling over each other to get out. "I know them all."

The pilots agreed that they needed someone who knew that locality.

"Have you ever flown before?" they asked, and he had to say no.

"Well, it doesn't matter," they said. "The older men haven't either. You will soon get adjusted." One helped him to fasten his safety belt. "You speak good English," they told Quiet Boy and he was glad.

"These are earphones," one of the crew explained, fastening them over the boy's head, then arranging his own. "We will need to talk to each other and to those in the other planes. The name of our pilot is Captain York."

"To Canyon de Chelly!" someone called out. The motors sputtered and whirred, and the plane turned and started down the runway to take off.

Quiet Boy felt a thrill when the plane left the ground. If the occasion had not been so serious, and the danger so grave, he would have enjoyed himself.

Other planes flew alongside while the men talked together. Quiet Boy wondered how the planes remained at the same distance apart so long without colliding. The crewmen were well trained he was sure. They fly like birds, he thought, like the squawking wild geese flying south in the fall of the year.

The men discussed their position. They knew this by means of the map and flight time, the boy decided. They seemed to work on the basis of minutes. He heard them say it is so far between certain points and how many minutes it would take to go from one point to another.

"We are passing over the reservation boundary now,"

the pilot presently said. "From now on it's up to you," and he looked at Quiet Boy. "You know where the people live."

Quiet Boy looked out over the country. It was a big country. He hadn't known it was so big, and this was all Navajo Land. He had never seen it from this height —almost, but not quite. He had seen it from the high mesa country and from the cliffs of Canyon de Chelly.

When the plane dipped low he could see a few hogans like ant dens scattered about. There were cattle and horses just standing around. "That is probably because they can't go on," he told the men. "They have broken through the crusted snow. All they can do is stand there."

When the sun came up strong he could see people carrying something green to the corrals, and he knew what it was. It was piñon and cedar branches for the sheep to eat. He had done it himself many times, but the snow had never been this bad nor lasted so long.

"Hay lift!" one of the crew shouted and the plane banked low while great bales of hay and supplies dropped from its belly.

The plane circled and came back and banked again, and Quiet Boy could see people running out of the hogans like ants toward the hay and sacks of canned milk and meat.

This frightened him. He wished they would not come

out so quickly, not until the packages had landed. Someone might get hurt, for the sacks were heavy and were falling a long distance.

"What do you think is needed most?" they asked him.

"Besides food, medicine," he told them. "Some are sick with the lung sickness and the flu. And some are very old and some very young. The babies need milk for they cannot eat, and the cows and milk goats may be snowed under or lost. At my own hogan penicillin is needed, and flu medicine."

The men sorted out the medicine and put it in some bags to drop. Quiet Boy was so happy that tears came to his eyes, but he brushed them away quickly.

Then they flew on north and east toward Canyon de Chelly. They called out names of many places the boy had heard of or knew about.

"Greasewood, Ganado, Chinle," they named for him, and in a way he knew where they were.

He saw some of the red bluffs and tall needlelike peaks of the Canyon de Chelly. The planes dipped and swooped like the great eagles and hawks he had seen. Sometimes the plane dipped and banked until Quiet Boy was sure it would turn completely over and spill them all out.

He knew that this deep, winding canyon was really three canyons in one, thirty miles long, with gorges a thousand feet deep in places. The sides were so steep and smooth that even the snow could not stick for long. The plane dropped down in an air pocket, five hundred feet, they told him, and Quiet Boy felt sick at his stomach. Someone gave him a paper bag and for a long time he was too occupied to look.

"It's all right," the crew told him. "We have all been sick at one time or another."

Then he felt better as the plane circled around for a while. He heard them say they were 18,000 feet high, and that was very high, but somehow he felt better up there above the clouds. It was when they were near the ground that he seemed to get sick, when the mountains or the trees went by so quickly.

"The fog is bad," he heard them say.

And it was so. The clouds began to look exactly like mountain ranges, and white sand dunes, and some looked like solid white mesas. He couldn't see the earth below now. He couldn't see through the clouds and they were too low to fly under. Down there was where his people were, under the fog and the clouds and the snow, and he couldn't help them. Perhaps they were starving and freezing, still he could not see them. He could not find his own hogan. He strained his eyes, but it was of no use. He could see nothing that looked familiar.

He had failed them. He had failed his own people, the Dineh, and the plane crew, and the Red Cross. He had failed the Army and Navy. And he had failed the government men.

"We will go back," the crew finally said. "back to Winslow. We can't do any more. This is it."

And they circled once more and went back.

What could he do now? He was not a man after all. He was a sheep's tail. He was a failure, lost and good for nothing. He was sick—very sick.

11: *Black Snow*

"WHY DON'T you eat?" the pilot of the plane asked Quiet Boy, as they sat in the restaurant with steaming plates of food before them. "Aren't you hungry? You should be." Captain York gave him a friendly look.

But Quiet Boy only sat and stared around. Yes, he should be hungry. Only yesterday, when he had stood at the window and looked in how he had wanted to be inside, inside this very place, at the Winslow Restaurant, sitting at a table like the other people with food before him! Now he was here and the food before him and he could not eat.

"Try to eat just a little," coaxed a good-natured crewman called Mack. "You need a little something in that stomach of yours. It looks mighty flat." He grinned.

"We leave in twenty minutes," another one said, looking at his watch. "We'll have just time enough to make one more trip before nightfall."

Quiet Boy took up a little of the roast beef on his fork then and put it in his mouth. It tasted like dead wood.

He tried to eat a little of the food the men had bought for him. At least he figured they would buy it. He couldn't pay for it, that was sure, unless they would take his wide concho belt for pay. He would hate to let it go, but he would. His people often traded like that. The white man's money had once had no appeal to Indians except for making jewelry or spearheads or bow guards. But, of course, that was long ago. The last few days he had realized how much money was really worth.

Slowly he began to eat, glad that he knew how to use a fork like the other men. His mother had a few forks and knives and spoons. Grandfather said they were just in the way, but he and Ti-wi and Nespah used them very well.

He wondered where he would go when the plane crew went back to the plane. Perhaps he could find Douglas or the man who gave him his breakfast. Perhaps he could get a job at the airport. "They need people for the construction work," the man had told him.

The plane crew talked a great deal about the storm, the situation of the Indians, and made plans for a return trip to Canyon de Chelly. But no names were mentioned. They hadn't said that he would go back. They probably wouldn't. He followed them to the cashier's desk, where the pilot and the clerk exchanged a few words and some slips of paper which didn't look at all like money. Then the men went out to the car that had brought them all in from the airport, and began to get in.

He was just turning to go on down the street to find Douglas, when the pilot spoke.

"Come here, Quiet Boy. Get in the front seat with me, I want to know more about your home country."

So he got in the car, in the front seat.

"Do I go back?" he asked.

"Of course." Mack thumped him heartily. "Don't give up with only one try. Try, try again," he said. "You did fine until the fog closed in."

"No use to worry," the other man told him. "The fog and clouds have cleared in the east. No doubt it will be better at Canyon de Chelly. We'll find your people this time, I think."

Quiet Boy instantly felt like a new man. He was going back to help his people. He could face anything now. He wished he had eaten more food, as he hitched his belt up a notch and touched the turquoise thunderbird in the wide buckle. He looked at the Sun-bearer and saw the great round ball shining brightly. How beautifully it glistened on the white snow! It was surely a good omen this time.

The plane was loaded and they took off, flying right back over the same route, except that this trip they could follow the black ribbon road cleared off by the snow-plow. Quiet Boy did not get plane sick this time. He watched carefully for the places he had seen before, chewing the gum they had given him.

"The gum is good for your ears," they told him, "and your stomach, too." They laughed and told a joke or two.

"During World War II," Mack told them, "a wounded soldier was put in a plaster cast from head to waist and put on a plane to be flown to another hospital. When all were aboard, the pilot explained how to use the life jackets and how to leave the plane if it had to be ditched. When he had finished, he asked if there were any questions. From the man in the plaster cast came this one. 'Pilot, when you all leave the plane, what would you like me to do with it?'"

Quiet Boy listened to their good humored talk, wondering what he himself would do if left on a plane. There were many buttons, switches, and gadgets to push and pull to control a plane. How could any one man remember which ones to use? These men he knew had had a lot of training. They were trustworthy or else they would not be flying—not under these difficult conditions.

When they reached Canyon de Chelly, things looked natural, though covered with snow as before. But the

Sun-bearer was at just the right position in the sky and the fog was almost gone.

Quiet Boy looked up at the few white clouds above and sent up a fervent prayer to the spirits to make sure the flight of the "great eagle," to make strong and steady the hands of the pilot, to aid the hay-lift men in dropping the supplies on the right spot, and to make keen his own senses that he might see and know his own hogan and help all the Dineh—his people.

"Over there! There is one, over there!" Quiet Boy cried. When he showed them the place the big plane circled lower, and the supplies were made ready to drop.

"Hay lift!" came the cry and he knew it was done.

"Is that your home?" the pilot asked as they circled back to check.

"No, not my home. It is—the hogan of—Tall Boy," Quiet Boy said.

He could see Tall Boy's black-and-white pinto with many other horses standing in the snow. When the plane circled so that they could check again, he saw the pony reach out his long neck toward the hay that was scattered all about.

"Where to now, Quiet Boy?" a crewman asked, as the plane leveled off.

"To the left a little, by that red peak. Drop food and fuel."

The plane circled and the drop was made.

"Say, what's going on here?" the crewman asked. "That looks like only an abandoned old car out there, not a hogan."

"Yes," said Quiet Boy, "a rusty old black car. But I think there is a man in it. He uses it to drive about the country, stealing sheep, maybe. That's how he makes a living, I think."

"What? Stealing sheep?" Captain York looked at him strangely, questioningly.

"It is the Navajo way," Quiet Boy explained slowly. "That is, I mean—not to let a man freeze, not any man, not even a thief. He is a bad man. I think he knows I know at last, but he picked me up in the blizzard."

The man studied him for a moment.

"Now where is your hogan? Hadn't we better try there next, with your little sister sick?" he asked.

"There is one other first," Quiet Boy told them. "It's right on our way." And as they dipped and banked he saw plainly the words on the snow made with green piñon boughs laid together:

DROP FOOD HERE, MANY GOATS.

"I didn't see any goats at all," the crewman said, scanning the area below after the food had been dropped.

"That is the man's name," Quiet Boy explained. "He was my father's buddy in the war. Only, Many Goats came back, with just one leg, yes, but he came back. My father didn't make it."

The plane men were silent, and Quiet Boy wondered if he had said or done something wrong.

"There it is! That is my hogan!" he cried. "To the left of the gully wash. There is the arroyo. That's where Gogo is." He could see the place he knew so well. It was like a model he had seen at the fair once.

"Drop hay in the arroyo?" the man asked, not being able to see the little mound called a hogan, covered as it was with snow, or the shelter for the sheep. He was looking at the windmill three miles away, standing like a beacon signal, reaching up out of the snow, its flag pointing with the wind.

"Not at the windmill, nor in the arroyo. The hogan is to the left and not too far, about a half minute away," Quiet Boy directed.

"Hay lift!" the drop man shouted, and down went bales of hay, looking smaller and smaller.

"Now circle and drop the food and the medicine packages." The man spoke into the mike, and the plane began to turn again.

Quiet Boy watched carefully, but no one came out of the hogan. The snow lay undented. There was not a stir, not when the plane was overhead, not even after the plane was soaring away again. His heart froze.

"Perhaps it is too late." His voice was unsteady. They might all be dead from the flu. They might be frozen. He sighed heavily. Captain York questioned him, and he told him more about Ti-wi, who was ill, about Grandfather, Nespah and Atchee.

A sick sensation surged through Quiet Boy's tired body. He wouldn't, couldn't bear to go on thinking. The plane dipped and banked, rose and dipped again and again.

"Check," he heard someone say as bale after bale of hay dropped—food, medicine.

"Check," he heard the answer again and again, and then everything changed—from very white to very dark. Even the snow was black.

12: *The Gift*

"YOU HAVE been very sick," Quiet Boy heard a soft voice say when he awoke.

He blinked his eyes and turned his head a little. He saw the woman standing there in a white uniform. Her cap was white, too, as white as little Runt's curly coat, as white as the snow outside. She looked a lot like the school nurse.

"You are in the hospital," she told him. "Captain York brought you here. He said to tell you when you woke that your people are all right. The snowplow got through to them with the doctor soon after you dropped the packages. Now go back to sleep for a while, that is, if you are sleepy."

He was. But it was no time at all until he was awakened again.

"Now take your medicine, and you shall have some lunch." The nurse was shaking him, "you haven't actually eaten in a long time." She was soon spooning food into his mouth. "You had food just the same," she went on.

He wondered how he could have had food, yet not eaten. Then she showed him the instruments at his bedside with the jug of liquid and the long tube, and explained how the glucose went through his veins to feed him.

"You have had the flu for three days and still have it," She patted his arm. "You and your people have been through a hard time. But thanks to all the pilots and crewmen of the hay lift, to the police, the Red Cross, the doctors and the new miracle drugs, the Army and Navy, it is not as bad as it might have been, and you yourself will be up and around in no time."

Quiet Boy's head was clearing and he began to remember all that had happened.

"May I come in?" asked a gruff yet friendly voice one morning, and there was the big policeman wheeling himself into the room in a wheel chair.

"Sure." The nurse smiled. "Now I'll just leave you two old cronies together, and go see that new patient." She took a fever thermometer out of Quiet Boy's mouth, wrote something in a notebook and went out.

"I am sorry I couldn't keep my word that day—a week ago now." The policeman was apologizing— apologizing to Quiet Boy. "When you told me about Black Chiddi, I was sure he was the thief I was looking for. But he got me first—from the back. The bullet hit me in the right leg and I couldn't follow him. The snow had been bad, but it helped us all, including you, to catch the rascal. Captain York radioed in that you had spotted the sheep stealer stranded in the snow. Black Chiddi was almost frozen when the snowplow and the sheriff reached him."

Quiet Boy's eyes got larger and larger. He sat up in bed. Black Chiddi was caught at last, the sheep of the Dineh—his people—were safe! Not many Navajos were troublemakers. There had been very few since the Dineh had agreed with Kit Carson long ago to make peace, to war no more. Only Black Horse and a few others had made trouble about the schools. Black Chiddi had been very much like Black Horse.

"And that's not all," the policeman went on. "In the back of his car were three sheep still alive. They belonged to an Indian named Many Goats, and were promptly returned to him, of course. Black Chiddi is in the jail hospital, awaiting sentence, and there is a reward from which you will get your share." Quiet Boy wondered about this reward and what he would do with his.

Someone else came into the room then, just as the policeman wheeled himself out. It was Tall Boy this time. How glad Quiet Boy was to see someone from his own home area, even though it was Tall Boy.

"I sorry you sick," Tall Boy began shyly. He spoke English out of respect for the *pelicani* hospital. "They say you fly the great eagle, drop food, hay for my pinto pony. I do not deserve. I been bad but I not kill Gogo, I not that bad. I take only Little Runt, ride along with Black Chiddi in car that once. I tell policeman where Little Runt is, and many more sheep Black Chiddi take. I bring kid back to your hogan. I go now, but I your friend. Nurse say not stay long, good-by." And he was gone.

Tall Boy had confessed, just as Grandfather had said the Dineh used to do long ago. Tall Boy was changed. Tall Boy was now his friend, and Little Runt was alive. How happy Ti-wi would be, and how happy he himself was, too!

It was an exciting time at the hospital for Quiet Boy as he improved, and as the storm cleared. He could see the Sun-bearer shining brightly outside. It was a good omen for sure now. It had been all along. It just took time, that was all, and patience. One just needed to be very patient. "The time will come," Grandfather had said, and it had.

There were letters and cards of sympathy from friends and strangers all over the country. There was a get-well card from Mr. Marshall and the faculty at the school. Miss Burns' name headed the list. How happy he would be to go back to school.

The family of Many Goats came to see him. "You

have done well," Many Goats told him. "Ditsa Toddy would be proud." And Quiet Boy knew a great content.

He glanced at Yellow Corn who had been so good. All during the illness of Ti-wi, he heard she had helped his mother. And there was Dancing Eyes. How glad he was to have done his part, hunting for her and finding her safe that day in the gully wash! Pepe gave him a green taw marble.

"I have many more," his friend told him.

"Thanks," Quiet Boy said, knowing this one was Pepe's favorite taw.

Then he glanced shyly at Doli. She had never been so pretty, and she had the kindest eyes!

Chief White Cloud came to see him, also.

"A true Dineh," he said to Quiet Boy. "One of the people. When you are well again, I shall take you for the first time to the Tribal Council. We need men like you to help plan the government."

"Thank you, my chief," Quiet Boy said gravely. But his heart was dancing with gladness. His father, too, had been on the Tribal Council.

As he lay in bed he thought of all the things that had happened to him, and of the ways of the people, and of the big world. Some of the ways were good ways and some were not. It was the people mostly that made the different ways. Some were good and some were bad.

Some of the people and their ways changed for the better, and some never did. It was the same with the Navajos and with the white people. Many of their ways had fused. Many of their trails were the same trails now.

Yes, even the white men and their ways had changed, and like the Navajos they yearned for the old ways they saw departing, never to come back. Some of the white people even resented the changing ways and would never accept them completely. In that, they were like Grandfather, and Quiet Boy's heart softened, for he loved the Ancient One.

The days passed quickly, especially when Quiet Boy grew stronger, and people came and went.

But the best part was a visit from his own family, Nespah, Ti-wi, Atchee and even Grandfather. The little group came in, beaming.

"Already we have another sheep dog," Atchee told him.

"He is only a puppy. It is for you to train him," Ti-wi said, still looking a little peaked from her illness.

"Mr. McClure, the agent, brought him," Nespah added.

The Ancient One hobbled in with a large package under his arm.

"Gift!" he grunted. And Quiet Boy knew that was the only English word his Grandfather had ever spoken.

When he opened the package there was what Quiet Boy wanted most, and never expected to get, not from Grandfather.

"A radio!" he cried, and a tear fell on the Ancient One's hand.